LAST NIGHT IN BRIGHTON
آخر ليلة في برايتون

Ghorba Ghost Story Series, Part Two
سلسلة قصة شبح الغربة: الكتاب الاخير

Massoud Hayoun
مسعود حيون

 **DARF PUBLISHERS**

Darf Publishers, 2022
277 West End Lane
West Hampstead
London, NW6 1QS

Last Night in Brighton by Massoud Hayoun

The moral right of the author has been asserted

Cover designed by Luke Pajak

ISBN Paperback: 9871850773504
ISBN eBook: 9781850773511

Contents

لنادية

For Nadia

زوروني كل سنه مرة
حَرام تنسوني بالمرة

سيد درويش الاسكندراني

Visit me once a year
It would be a shame if you suddenly forgot me
Sayed Darwish, the Alexandrian

1. The Yawn التثاؤب

If I was in Brighton Beach, Brooklyn, I was partying on my own. In the celebratory sense, yes. But also, I'd probably smoked a little weed. And if I was out of weed, I'd taken one or five shots at a Russian restaurant on the boardwalk. That's because, if I was in Brighton — which I often was — it didn't just happen. I couldn't just will myself there. I had to get there physically, on an hour-long express train from Manhattan, and then mentally, to the spiritual space of Beach House ballads and Costco buttercream cakes. Coat my insides in crushed velour and luxury.

It was the weed that night, at first. Premium. Sensuality, once more.

As usual, I went at dusk, before the shops closed. The sky was a clement, monotone periwinkle at that hour. The ocean matched the sky, of course. That's science.

I stood in the ocean, up to my knees in murky, sudsy waves, and I felt the half-hearted clemency of low-tide rush over me. I liked to see the periwinkle of that hour against the grey and brick backdrop of the austere Soviet-style flat blocks. Those buildings signified to me that we are small, in our little cubbies, that only when we are together do we have any heft. I liked to half-see the Coney Island Parachute Jump — the lit-up Bethlehem steel skeleton of a once-great and gaudy attraction — glow in the distance, closer to the Coney Island subway station where I typically arrived, alone, and walked a couple of miles up the coast, to Brighton.

That April evening, someone in charge of the lights at Coney Island had set the still and skeletal Parachute Jump in the colours of the American flag, in the way maintenance staff likely put lipstick on Mao, Lenin, and Evita's embalmed, slowly festering corpses. I was about two miles up the coast from the Parachute Jump when I was partying alone in Brighton. And yet I could see it shimmering in the distance. I was not on the Parachute Jump when I was in Brighton, but I was often in free fall. That's life.

This was a farewell party.

I regretted, suddenly, that I was high. I felt an urge to remember. Everything would change the next day.

A man on the boardwalk cycled past, a few yards from where I stood in the ocean. I could hear his bicycle tires dancing along the boardwalk planks, and overlaying that, the sound of a radio speaker, probably in his backpack. It played Will You Still Love Me Tomorrow? by the Shirelles.

A little too perfect, I thought, but still poetic enough that I should write it down somewhere. That's the predicament of the pot smoker, isn't it? You have all these powerful, profound thoughts and emotional moments, and even if you have the courage to collect yourself and write them down, they depreciate in value when you sober up and read them over. Slippery thing, meaning.

I was not, to be sure, like the protagonist of that song — a sorrowful woman. I am not as she was, begging for tonight to spill over into tomorrow. In fact, I'd already done my best to make certain it would not.

Kashkar Cafe was not far from the shoreline, in reality. But time played tricks when I was high. It either sped up or slowed down. When it sped up, that meant I was high enough to forget from one minute to the next that I had been walking from my habitual starting-off point, knee-deep in the waves at Brighton Beach, to Kashkar Cafe. It meant I was too high to care very much about where I was going. If I wasn't high enough, I'd remember on occasion the forgotten moments from before, and I would feel like I had been walking the same road for an eternity, locked in a haze, like a spiritual prison.

It is a sin to wish your life away, but if I had my druthers, time would have always sped up, on the road to Kashkar. Britney Spears said in an interview once that the secret to happiness is a bad memory. I agree. I wanted to forget where I've come from, so the trek would be easier. And I was able to choose, horrific as it may seem, to live in a state of perpetual amnesia. I was a constitutionally unsentimental and unafraid person. I did not attend my high school, undergraduate, or masters graduation ceremonies. I never kept in touch with my schoolmates. Or former work colleagues. I liked a good, clean break. No cooing goodbyes. I was tired of those. Nothing precious. No time.

At least for me, pot can have a number of side effects. Of course, there's the hunger, which is another reason why I prefer a quick hike over to Kashkar Cafe. And then, there is the worst possible outcome of 420 — the reverse of my intentions: The pot magnifies my usual anxiety ten-fold and seals it with newfound paranoia — the mother of all side effects. Ironically, that night I had taken my pot in the form of a little chocolate biscuit, to calm me.

I wondered if I had made a grave mistake. Standing beneath the metro overpass, the sound of the express Q train rushing overhead drove up my heart rate, until I felt myself locked in a fit of frenzy. I squatted down, back against the wall of some bank. I held my head in my hands until the train passed. When I heard the sounds of relative calm, I looked around. To my left, a few metres away, was a rotund woman with a short, bouffant hairdo. She wore a tight black and grey Justin Bieber shirt from one of the Brighton discount clothing shops over a short, frilly, rainbow-coloured skirt. She smoked a long, thin lady cigarette, back against the wall. She looked up at the subway overpass that had become the bane of her existence, with its near-constant noise. I wanted her release. I wanted to see the hot air expel from my chest and disappear. I felt the urge. I had been a smoker for a decade until recently, until the cigarettes and I had abandoned each other, and I came to feel on occasion as though there was a little phantom limb between my index and middle fingers.

I yawned. I felt a profusion of oxygen — mixed with the roadside smog and some of the woman's second-hand smoke — inflate my lungs. The urge subsided. Like magic. I marvelled at how simple it had been. A little yawn.

In a moment's lucid salvation, I recalled Kashkar Cafe. I recalled that I was hungry and that Kashkar was located several blocks to my right, past a synagogue, a few markets, and a surrealist pastry shop that serves cream cakes by the self-service slice. Cakes with all the whimsy of the psychedelic onion-shaped domes atop St. Peters Basilica. A great many things could pull me aside en route to Kashkar, high as I was. That evening, I stayed the course. It took unusual commitment, but I pulled myself together and moved onward.

What awaited me on the other side of my journey were meaty, little parcels of something resolutely in-between: Dumplings with noodle dough in the Chinese style, filled with a Turkic sort of seasoned lamb, topped with dill and served with sour cream to suit the Slavic and other post-Soviet palettes of that neighbourhood. Maybe that's why I love Kashkar Cafe. It was a borderland like Tijuana — a place where all the road signs point elsewhere. A place full of dissatisfied people with the courage to abandon the past for a vast and violent unknown. That night had been a borderland between the me of that day and the next. It was a fitting last supper.

2. Regression للتراجع

'You think I'm bullshitting you,' she said.

He did.

'I'm here, aren't I? I paid upfront,' he replied. He wanted to sound confident in his decision, but he had not slept the night before, and his feet were tired. He wanted to spread his toes, but his shoes were full of sand. He hoped she wouldn't notice little grains of it on her wooden floors. He reckoned he looked like a ghost — or worse, a drug addict — large, puffy circles under his eyes. But then again, maybe she was used to this class of people — the ghost and/or junkie class of people. Half-living people.

'Because if you actively disbelieve it, it won't work,' she continued. 'Because I can't guarantee your satisfaction.'

'What does that mean?' he asked, a bit worried.

'It means that if you don't get there, that's on you,' she answered, looking at him with intent, motherly eyes. 'No refunds.'

He looked her in the face. She had a strange twitch — a nervous, little seizure in her left eye, barely perceptible.

'I made a very clear decision,' he assured her. After a moment's quiet, he continued: 'No refunds. I am aware of the possible pitfalls, Doctor Fahmy.'

'I'm not a doctor,' Doctor Fahmy said. 'I need you to be fully aware of what's happening for legal purposes. I am a hypnotherapy practitioner. You can call me Lana.'

'I would feel more comfortable calling you Doctor Fahmy,' he said. Doctor Fahmy frowned. A moment passed.

'Alright, Lana,' he conceded.

'Alright, we'll begin with the formalities,' Doctor Fahmy said. She stood and escorted him from the sofa in her narrow foyer through her kitchen to a small pantry she had converted into a makeshift office with the help of some Ikea furniture. He reclined on a chaise lounge. On one side of the chaise hung a framed diploma from Jackson Heights Hypnotherapy Institute, and below it was a small bookshelf of self-help titles. Doctor Fahmy sat on an armchair on the other side of the chaise. On a small desk beside her armchair was a notepad, paper, a pen, and some spectacles.

'Would you like a blanket?' she asked.

'No, it's hot outside — Why do you ask?' he returned. She had offered him a blanket in their previous session, which had been their first, but he felt uncomfortable asking why. He was still irritable from that session. An expected side effect.

'It comforts some people,' she said. 'That's another point I'd like to get over to you: The purpose of this is to find answers. Finding answers comes at the cost of living in blissful ignorance, right? What you are about to experience may bring up some trauma for you. That pain is not only natural, it can be a goal. A healing crisis. Ultimately, what we're about to do here together today is about addressing how things stuck in the distant past are still informing and obstructing the present.'

'You're not responsible,' he said, hurrying her.

Doctor Fahmy nodded. 'You have signed paperwork to that effect and are completely aware of what you have signed. You are aware that I am recording the audio of this session. You are fully conscious of your decisions and are under no form of duress. You are free to leave anytime,' she said. He inspected the room. There was a large tape recorder from the 1990s sitting on the floor, in the corner of her pantry-office. Doctor Fahmy reached out her hand to signal that he should respond to her disclaimers verbally.

'Yes, I consent to all of this of my own free will,' he said, unsettled by the recording device.

'You are also acknowledging that your requested treatment is non-standard. We have worked out the details. You have agreed to and pre-paid your fees,' she said. He nodded. She lifted a hand signalling him to speak.

'Yes,' he said.

'The treatment you are about to receive is, per our discussions prior to this session, not Past Life Regression Therapy,' she continued. 'You are about to undergo an amended Past Life Regression Therapy. It is tailored to your specific requests. What you are about to experience should more accurately be called just a Time Regression Therapy. It employs many of the same techniques of my Past Life offerings, but the purpose is to travel to a space at once familiar and unknown to you.'

He asked for a glass of water. In the minute it took her to retrieve it from the adjacent kitchen, thoughts raced through his mind. He had already paid several hundred dollars for this session. He could leave. He realised that once he had entered a state of hypnosis with Doctor Fahmy, it would be difficult for him to rouse himself to a fully conscious waking state. What sort of pain? he wondered. Does anyone not come back from a Past Life Regression therapy? Surely not — It would be all over the news: MAN DIES IN (BULLSHIT) HYPNOTHERAPY SESSION. What if the emotional trauma of such a thing is so severe that the person who returns is only a fraction of who they had been? He quieted his thoughts. If he shared any of these doubts with Doctor Fahmy, she would have refused to treat him. He had come too far. He thought about his first session, which had been a remarkable success. Doctor Fahmy handed him a glass of lukewarm tap water. He downed it and placed the glass on the floor beside his chaise lounge.

'The sensations you are about to experience are true to life. Some say their experiences in that state are as vivid as this reality. Sometimes they are even more intense than your life here and now. There is a great deal of disagreement among practitioners about what it is that you will experience — whether it's simply what exists in your subconscious or an alternate dimension. Of course, there are things that are not explained by science. Scientists themselves are the first to say that they arrive at a certain point, and beyond that point is an inexplicable divine, always just out of reach of our comprehension. Within the study of physics there are a great many proponents of the idea of parallel universes or parallel realities. There is some possibility that what you are about to experience will affect another reality. It is also not unthinkable that after our session, you will feel yourself to have returned to a reality very different to the one you are experiencing now. In my view, as a hypnotherap ist, there are no hard and fast answers. You decide the significance of the world you are about to enter. Upon return to this — or that — reality, you may experience feelings of depression or thoughts of suicide. You bear responsibility for seeking the necessary professional help if you experience these emotions. The intent of our undertaking, however, is to resolve issues and hopefully set you on track to healthier, more mindful living. Is that clear?'

He nodded. A moment passed until he recalled the recorder. 'Yes,' he said aloud.

'What are the objectives of your requested Time Regression Experience?' she asked. 'What is it about your present that you are trying to fix?'

'I'd rather not say, if that's alright,' he said. She paused again. 'As you say, it's for me to deal with how these experiences impact whatever life is like after our session,' he said.

'Fair enough. Hypnotherapy is indeed mostly a solo enterprise. I can lead the horse to water, so to speak, with the tools I've received in my training. But if you don't actively believe in and want to undertake this journey, you'll just be a man in a chair in Bay Ridge, Brooklyn in 2019,' she said.

'Why was there none of this preamble for our first session?' he asked.

She paused.

'That was a very different sort of session. This is the protocol for a non-standard session,' she said. He nodded.

'I brought a photograph. I'm not sure if it's any use to you,' he said.

'It's not necessary, but you may hold it, if it makes you feel more comfortable,' she said.

He felt discomforted by her insistence that he get

comfortable. He had not brought the photo to serve as a security blanket. He brought it as an object to lead the way to back to the dead. He had read once in high school, for AP World History, about the Egyptian Book of the Dead. He read that there were several writings out of Ancient Egypt that described the path from the world of the living to the afterlife. Those journeys involved amulets and spells and all of the deceased's riches, packed into the colossal monuments to mourning that are the pyramids of his and Doctor Fahmy's most distant ancestors. Where Doctor Fahmy saw a security blanket, he saw a photographic amulet. He assumed that Doctor Fahmy, in Bay Ridge, in the enclave of Egyptian and other Arab Americans who live in that space, would have recognised the photo for what it was. He was disappointed that she had not. But he could not show it. He would not turn back.

'May I see the photo?' she asked. He handed it to her.

' حاجة حلوة، الصورة دي! ' - Haga helwa, elsoura di, she said - What a beautiful photo!

'I think a great many people would like to experience what you're about to experience,' she continued. 'They just haven't asked or encountered anyone willing help them. I suppose my methods are a little out-of-the-box, even for hypnosis. How do you feel?'

Sam looked into Doctor Fahmy's face. He noticed her eye twitch as he had before. A sign of anxiety. The sort of small muscles that he reckoned caused crow's feet seized up and then released, seized up and then released.

'Does it matter?' he asked her. And then, realising that he was being disagreeable, he felt contrite. 'I'm sorry,' he offered

Doctor Fahmy. 'It's the withdrawal, and I'm overcome with nerves, as you can imagine.'

'You are about to return to the people in this photo,' she said. 'We are about to undertake something new and intrepid for us both. I absolutely understand the tension. But we have to march adroitly into this, or it won't work.'

Doctor Fahmy explained that she would count backward from 10 and that by the time she had arrived at 1, he would exist decades ago, across an ocean and a sea, in a land of great, big triangular monuments to mourning.

As she counted, Sam felt his hand dig into the chaise lounge armrest, like his seat was about to take off for flight. He turned his face from Doctor Fahmy so she would not see tears roll down his cheek. He was afraid that she — or he — would misinterpret them as tears of sorrow and stop.

3. Falafel فلافل

They said Mamoun's in Downtown Manhattan served the best falafel place in New York. That's saying something in a city with an Egyptian falafel cart on every corner.

At the time, I lived on the Lower East Side, not far from St. Mark Place, the street full of bars, crust punks, tattoo parlours, and Mamoun's — a little out of place, like a warm embrace. I would have sooner gone to Brighton that night too, but the express train wasn't running. I didn't choose Mamoun's; Mamoun's came to me at the right time. I began wandering Alphabet City, then I headed downtown through Nolita and Chinatown, then West through Soho and around Greenwich Village, then back east toward St. Mark's and Mamoun's. I passed what must have been at least a hundred restaurants, many of them serving good and affordable food. I was hungry and tired. I felt my blood sugar descending. But frustratingly, I couldn't settle on a place for dinner. Everything was wrong.

Before I arrived at Mamoun's, I realised why I was being so maddeningly indecisive. That's what happens when you wander about town like that, like a pained soul. You sort things out in your head. That's why I habitually came to Brighton high or hammered: to stop my constant self-interrogation, where I was both the good and bad cops.

I realised that night on St. Marks, probably at the very

moment the chef dropped my falafel into the deep fryer, that I was still hungry like a human, but I was beyond food. The body functioned; the soul, or whatever it is in us that produces appetite and taste, did not. I had lost my flavour for living.

I had never been to Mamoun's before that night, much as I had heard about it. I had spent much of my life not eating fattening and greasy foods, in part to make myself beautiful enough for a Hollywood romance that merited what is heavy for me about being gay. Even growing up, we seldom ate falafel, because I was raised by my grandparents, who suffered from conditions of the heart. By the time I was born, our family was already beyond the deliciousness they had known. That's what happens when you are raised by old people who, in turn, were raised by young people, without the same concerns about longevity: From the start, you are raised on reminiscences. Nothing seems to happen in realtime. Gone before my time were the days of falafel, their heft, their cholesterol. Cherished in the rearview were the youthful falafel, like the time-before land from whence we came, like Egypt.

That night, I stopped caring about any of it — about my heart, about being fat or greasy or too far from home. There was a sainted stillness in me. An indulgence.

I did not order a sandwich. I'd have loved a sandwich, to be sure, with an oven-baked pita, fresh salad, pickles, and tahina. But I wanted to really taste the falafel. I was uncertain I would even recall its flavour, since I had kept myself from it for so long. I ordered three à la carte orders of falafel, four nuggets per order. The cashier offered tahina on the side for dipping. 'No thank you,' I said, anticipating a reaction.

The cashier looked down at the register with a grimace, as if to say I was foolish. We both knew: Tahina is a marvel of the Arab traditions of culinary and scientific innovation. Our pioneering and imaginative ancestors had performed a kind of alchemy — They had conjured a cream from sesame seeds. But I had come for falafel, not tahina. I had come to settle a score with falafel.

Mamoun's was a crowded establishment, not just because the falafel are among the best in the United States, but because New York City restaurants — like New York City flats — are small. You always have to slide into a seat with your ass in other diners' faces. That night, I wedged myself into a spot at the window-side table, between a beautiful, fat woman with very small pores who was entirely unconcerned with me as she enjoyed the sensual experience of her sandwich and an straight couple with unimpressive faces who had already finished their meal and, in their otherworldly canoodling, had neglected to yield their space to the hungry people waiting for seats.

I counted 12 falafel. I lifted one to behold it. I bit into it and marvelled at the innards — the way the parsley in the falafel batter had yielded such a dazzling emerald-tinted nugget. The perfect taste. Not too much grease. With other non-Egyptian falafel I had eaten in the past, I lamented the use of chickpeas in place of the Egyptian fava bean, our life source, our shit in the figurative sense, and literally, since it was the main source of fibre in our Egyptian-American diets. But Mamoun's non-Egyptian falafel was beyond reproach. My eyes began to cross as I inspected the insides for whatever it was that made them so delicious. I realised I would never make another falafel again, with fava or chickpeas. I popped it into my mouth. And then I put another into my mouth and another, until my cheeks were full, and I was forced to breath through my nose. I was uncertain whether the sensation of occlusive moisture on my face was grease or my tears. My eyes began to burn, so I closed them. I popped another falafel in my mouth. A groan — a gust of air, like a door creaking — came forth from somewhere in my chest. Rather loud, I immediately recognised it as having come from a place of despair. A release.

When I opened my eyes, the straight couple were staring and smiling.

'You alright, buddy?' the man asked.

I looked at him blankly, until it became apparent that he should look away.

Six falafel remained. I put my hand in my plate. I wanted to feel the falafel grease. I wanted to know the oil intimately. I could feel the straight man looking at me timidly out of the corner of his eye. Of its own volition, my hand seemed to wrap around the remainder of the falafel in their little paper basinet, strangling them out of shape, back into a state resembling the batter from which they came. This child's food-play had become a performance for the straight man. Then I began to ball the batter again. Slowly. Muscle memory. I had only ever made falafel once. And that was all it took. I would remember the motions of it for the rest of my life.

I was certain now that I was crying, as a tear rolled down my cheek, cutting through the sweat and grease on my face. I should have been ashamed. I was miserable as ever. But I was also happy. It had been some time since I could cry.

When I had prepared the reconstituted falafel, I used the clean back of my right hand — for I am an old-fashioned gentleman — to nudge it over to the straight man who had manifestly been waiting for the climax of our time together. I arose and walked to the door. I wondered as I left if I was the weirdest person the straight couple encountered that evening on St. Marks.

' صحة وهنا ' - Saha wa hana, I had leaned down and told the straight people, as I passed through the exit beside them. To your health.

4. Exodus מصر יציאת

I never anticipated I would even want to go back, until I could not. So maybe I deserve exile. I squandered my chance.

I had not slept much the night before. When I woke, the sun had risen over the pyramids, visible so clearly in the distance from my little hotel room in Giza. I left the room tidy. I did not want to leave a bad impression. The door was heavy. It closed with a thud. Then whatever mechanisms lock the door electronically — incomprehensible to me, who had never been good with tech — made a little hiss, and it was done. Sealed. The cab to Downtown Cairo sputtered along grand motorways with what felt like a dozen lanes, wrapping around large apartment buildings and a frenzy of billboards for Lipton Tea and politicians. The cabby offered me a Cleopatra cigarette. With my sallow, mournful, unrested face and bloodshot eyes, I must have looked like I needed a cigarette. I thanked him and inspected it before putting it in my mouth. He seemed to have ripped off the filters. *Go hard*, I thought, with appreciation.

'You're headed to the airport shuttle?' he asked, speeding along. I noticed his teeth were the colour of dried tobacco leaves.

I nodded. I looked away, out the window, at the frenzy of Cairo on its way to work, my arm perched on the windowsill. If I could have known it would be my last time, I would have stared more intently and made mental notes of everything. I would have filled my pockets with dirt.

'I was visiting my grandfather who raised me,' I said.

'Why were you at a hotel then?' the cabby asked. 'And why is your Arabic accent so poor?'

I rifled through my carry-on backpack, sitting between my feet. I withdrew my smartphone and pulled up a photo of my grandfather Wassim.

'He left Egypt when he was my age,' I told the cab driver. 'He never came back.'

'My goodness. He was handsome, wasn't he?' the cabby exclaimed.

'You mean to say I look like a steaming pile of trash, by comparison,' I said. We laughed. I wasn't offended. I am happy to be ugly by comparison.

'So you came here alone?' the cabby asked.

'I came here to see him. I dreamt I would meet him here again' , I said.

'I'm sorry — I'm afraid I don't really understand,' the cabby said.

'I had a dream. In the dream, his ghost was waiting for me in Egypt,' I said.

'And what happened?' the cabby said, suddenly very serious.

'I didn't find him,' I replied. 'He's dead.' The cabby nodded.

I flicked my cigarette butt out the window. I saw it in the rearview, little sparks as it tumbled back wards.

'What can I say?' I continued. 'My dreams are misleading. I guess I'm not psychic' .

'Thank Heaven,' the cabby said. 'Who wants to know the future?'

'Thank Heaven.'

My trip to Egypt had almost cost me my life. Maybe I would have seen my grandfather Wassim if that were the case. But I do thank Heaven I don't have the foresight to have known how difficult that trip would be, or I wouldn't have gone. And if I had not gone back at that moment in my life, I would have never seen it at all — the time-before land. Not in this reality, at least.

There were just a few people on the airport shuttle bus in the very particular situation of needing to catch a flight from a much smaller airport than Cairo International, an airport several hours north. There was a single empty seat next to me. Twice, in between surveying the large expanses of nothing, punctuated on occasion by some fields, a little hamlet, a small and stately mosque, I put my hand on the arm rest between us, my palm facing upward, fingers parted where his hand would have been.

I thought about Passover during the three hour bus ride. Jewish Egyptian people frequently use the term Exodus when they describe how we were made to leave Egypt after the occupation of Palestine in 1948. The Passover comparisons are a bit overdone, but it is indeed worth a moment's amusement that since time immemorial, our ancestors celebrated a holiday marking the Jewish departure from Egypt while we were a part of that land and that people. Several things, beyond Egypt and my departure from it, struck me as a kind of Passover in that moment. First, the Passover liturgy says specifically that in each generation, we must see ourselves as going out of Egypt. And then was the fact that customarily, Jewish families — not just

Egyptian — set an empty place for the Prophet Elijah at the Passover table. I was predisposed by my faith to nourishing things I cannot see or hold. I felt embarrassed for having come to Egypt. And yet the cabby that morning seemed to have understood the undertaking, even if he had never had the privilege of enough disposable income to go on a long international flight, chasing ghosts and dreams.

Only as the bus driver turned into the airport — Borg el Arab — did I discover that it was located just outside of the Alexandria city gate, built in a Greek style, with grandiose columns and the city name in Arabic and Greek. It was a cruel and unexpected coincidence. I had meant to travel to Alexandria, to the street where Wassim lived. I never made it there because of my fucking mental fragility.

In the airport waiting area, there was a bride fully prepared to get married upon our descent to my connecting flight in Dubai. She looked like a cream cake — lace and chiffon cascading from head to toe. She sweated like a pastry in a bakery window, her frosted makeup running like watercolour paints. She was trapped and suffocating in what was meant to be a place of joy. That was how I found Egypt, until I realised I could not go back, years after that departing flight.

A man on that plane to Dubai took the small, stale Arab bread the Emirates flight gave us, plastered it with butter and drizzled a packet of sugar on top, as you would have done. Only in that moment it occurred to me what a fool I had been to leave a place abundant with living memories of you. The most populous Arab nation, CNN always says.

At the end of the 1978 Egyptian film الصعود إلى الهاوية - El-Soud ila El-Hawiya - *Rise to the Abyss*, a traitor against the

Egyptian people who has sold national secrets to the nation's Western enemies realises the weight of what she has done when an intelligence agent repatriating her for trial tells her to behold the pyramids and the Nile.

'This is Egypt, madame,' he says.

Her face betrays a shot to the heart that prefigures her execution. My experience in that moment was similar, only it was not the pyramids or Nile that sobered me to my childish running from that exalted place, but an unhappy bride and a man making the best of a bad piece of pita — people like myself, taking the same ill-advised flight to a wealthy place.

5. Last Night تۇنۇگۇن كەچ

I fell into myself in the mirror at Kashkar Cafe's tiny bathroom, painted a Soviet pink, like many blocks of flats in North Korea and Russia's Far East. It was a stark, pale rose, dolling up a drab situation.

I felt as though I had been in the bathroom for an eternity. I was uncertain whether I was coming or going. *Had I peed? Should I pee?* In reality, I had only just arrived at Kashkar and was in the bathroom to wash my hands. Then I became transfixed by the size of my pores. My attention set on the pinkish hue of the whites of my eyes. I wondered if it was the weed or the pink walls reflected on my eyeballs that had turned my eyes that colour. I lost myself in my eyes for what felt like minutes, but who's to say how long it was? Time was taken by T.H.C.

I recalled the words of *Will You Still Love Me Tomorrow*. They came to me as a spoken word poem — no rhythm, just expressions of anxiety. The song had been a stray cat I had found out on the ocean that wandered into my head and curled up on a brainwave.

My reverie was suddenly shattered by an aggressive banging at the bathroom door that disappointed me greatly. I opened the door. A short, swarthy man, like Stalin without the moustache, awaited me there, speechless. In Kashkar Cafe, it was anyone's guess what language that man and I

31

spoke. So he indicated with his ice-cold stare that he was unamused by the great sojourn of self-loathing that I had undertaken in the bathroom, traveling through my vast pores to my bloodshot eyes.

I passed through a short corridor, peeked into the kitchen where a cleaver diced rice-stuffed intestines and a large stock pot sputtered. Syncopated rhythms produced a culinary musette. The dining room had filled since my self-eternity at the bathroom mirror. When I returned to what I recalled to have been my table, I found another man sitting there. I wondered then if I had ever been seated at all. I stood beside what I believed to have been my table, beholding its usurper for nearly a minute before he looked up and spoke.

'Sorry,' he said, not sorry enough for my liking. 'Busy night, I assume. I think they've doubled up tables.' British accent. Posh-sounding, from the little I know of British accents. He wore a brown corduroy jacket and a maroon patterned shirt, buttoned to the collar. A professor, I imagined. Not unhandsome. An explosion of lustrous, dark hair, like the unshorn wool of a black sheep. I wondered if he put raw egg or olive oil in his hair like my grandfather and I used to do before Shabbat, to make ourselves beautiful before Heaven.

'Sorry for staring. I wasn't sure if I was hallucinating,' I said. I had surprised myself with a cogent sentence. I must have been coming down. He smiled, I think. Or maybe he had scowled. I wondered if my 'Sorry' with a hard O sounded dreadful and classless to him. I was unsure whether my insecurity about my English was as a result of the weed or of my being an American encountering a British person.

I took a seat at the table, diagonal from him. A moment

later, I inspected my fidgeting hands in an effort not to stare at him as he closely inspected his menu's pictures of noodles, soups, dumplings, and pilaffs.

A waiter approached my table-mate, who pointed to one of the pictures on the menu and sat speechless.

' لەگمەن lagman, the waiter said, loudly and slowly. Fresh-pulled noodles.

'Yes, I'll have that, please,' the man said.

'Anything to drink?' the waiter asked. 'Tea?'

My table-mate thanked him.

My food arrived just before his. From the corner of my eye, I saw my table-mate stare into his dish, inspecting it. Then he twisted some of the long noodles around his fork. He seemed to chew for a particularly long time. He put his fork down and looked forward. I must have stared a little too obviously, because he turned to me and spoke:

'The foodie sites said to get the noodles.' he said.

'You disagree?' I asked, eyes glazed and mouth full.

'No, no — the noodles are nice,' he said. 'Maybe a little heavy.'

'Those noodles sit on my stomach,' I said.

A moment passed. I rose and pardoning the people behind me for knocking their chairs with my fumbling gait, spooned one of my large مانتی - manty- dumplings into my table-mate's plate, startling him.

'Oh thank you,' he said, stuttering a bit. 'That's not necessary.'

'I insist,' I said. 'This dumpling is the crown jewel of Brighton Beach, dumpling.'

The man smiled and nodded.

'Care for some sour cream and dill?' I asked. I never speak like that. Something about British people makes me speak like I have an audience with the Queen. I become ill-at-ease in my most fluent tongue, and I begin to effect a manner of speech that British people themselves would find pretentious. Like Madonna, after marrying Guy Ritchie, whose real British accent was very different to Madonna's imaginary one. I wonder if Guy Ritchie ever turned to Madonna in bed to say, 'I don't talk like that, innit?' I wonder if in her reckoning of their relationship, she was upstairs, and he was downstairs.

My table-mate ate my dumpling. He said nothing — just stared down into his plate, avoiding my gaze. *Ingrate*, I thought. I regretted sharing a table with him. And a dumpling. And Brighton Beach. I had naively given him too much of myself, all because he was a little handsome and charming, if only for his Britishness and his hair like a radiant crown of onyx.

He ate it with his fork turned downward onto his plate. Wassim, my grandfather, told me once that this was the British and therefore the correct way to eat. My grandfather venerated the British, like many Egyptian people continue to do. Wassim said British people feed themselves by pushing the food onto the back of a fork with their knife and balancing it into their mouths. I used a spoon to shovel my dinner into my pie hole.

'That has to be the most delicious thing I've ever tasted,' he said, finally.

'Really?' I asked, offering him my full and earnest heart. All it took was a moment's kindness to make me forget my resentment. He could have had the rest of my dumplings.

'One of the best, certainly,' he continued.

'I'd offer you some of this other dish, but maybe you won't like it?' I asked. 'It's lamb intestines, stuffed with flavoured rice.'

'Try me,' he said. 'I'm Mexican. We have menudo.'

'I thought you were British from the accent and the—' I said.

'And the?' he said, smiling.

'You're so well put together,' I said, smiling. I had meant to say that he looked unnecessarily well-dressed for a hole-in-the-wall eatery in southern Brooklyn.

'Thanks, I try,' he said. 'I'm half Mexican, raised in London.'

'So you're used to innards,' I said, passing him the چاسپ - chassip. He served himself two, which I thought was a bit cheeky of him.

'Exactly,' he said. 'So are you Uyghur or just some sort of connoisseur of Uyghur cuisine?'

'I'm Arab. Born here,' I said.

'In Brighton Beach?' he asked.

'I wish,' I answered. 'In the U.S. — here in New York. In Brooklyn. A short subway ride from here.'

'So you're a Brighton connoisseur,' he said.

'You could say that. I'm always here,' I answered.

'What's your name?' he asked.

'I'm Sam — Sam Saadoun, you?'

'I'm Brighton Arbuthnot. But I go by Tony, because…'

'Because Brighton Arbuthnot sounds like a bitchass name?'

'Woah!' he said, feigning shock and then smiling. 'I guess you got me there. Anyway, this is my first time.'

'At Kashkar?' I asked.

'Yes, and Brighton Beach — your American Brighton Beach anyway,' he said. 'I read about Kashkar Cafe and that Brighton Beach is an interesting place — a melange of different post-Soviet cultures, trapped in a time.'

'That's what they say — That it's like Russia in the 90's,' I said. 'I wouldn't know anything about those societies. But I do know that Brighton Beach is otherworldly. And other-timely. I know it's a subway ride from the city that, on the other side, feels like time travel.'

'That's beautiful,' Tony said.

'I could show you around Brighton,' I said. 'If you like.'

'I'd like that actually,' Tony said.

I looked down and smiled into my intestines.

And then suddenly, my smile faded, as quickly as one of the mask-changing performers in Chinese traditional 变脸 - bianlian novelty shows. In the final scene of the 1976 picture *Taxi Driver*, Robert De Niro's character, who is a Vietnam War veteran, looks into the rearview mirror of his cab and becomes disturbed. Some say it's because his improbable victory at the close of the film never happened. Some say it's because he sees what unknowable events occurred before the picture begins.

6. ONE واحد

'Ten
　　　'Nine
　　　　　'Eight
'You're falling deeper into yourself, Sam. When we reach
One, you'll begin to hear my voice more faintly, as you arrive
more clearly at your destination.
　　　　　　　　'Seven
　　　　　　　　　　'Six
　　　　　　　　　　　　'Five
'Almost there. Not much farther to go. Follow me, Sam —
　　　　　　　　　　　'Four
　　　　　　　　　　　　　'Three
　　　　　　　　　　　　　　　'Two
'ONE.'

'What you see before you is a corridor of doorways,' Doctor
Fahmy said. 'Tell me what you see.'

'A corridor of doorways,' Sam responded. 'It's not at all as
I expected.'

'What do you mean, Sam?' Doctor Fahmy asked. He
hesitated. 'Don't be shy,' she continued. 'What did you mean?'
He could hear her voice echoing as if over a loudspeaker.

'I had anticipated it would be more Egyptian — like the
Egyptian Book of the Dead,' he said. 'Ancient Egyptian
obstacles, life recast in frescoes on the walls of pyramids.'

'What do you see, Sam?' Doctor Fahmy asked.

'A dark corridor — No perceptible colour,' Sam said.

'Can you feel anything?' Doctor Fahmy asked. 'What do you feel, Sam?'

'Doorknobs,' he responded. 'I feel the metal.'

'Sam, historians have found that there are a great many Egyptian Books of the Dead,' Doctor Fahmy said. 'There were many Egyptian Books of the Dead commissioned for the deceased. The labyrinth you are in now may not have the aesthetic trappings you had expected, born in the U.S. and looking back at Egypt through American visions of what Egypt was. But you need to forget all that. What you see is indeed an Egyptian Book of the Dead, if only because you are an Egyptian on your way through to the realm of the dead. Tell me about the doors, Sam. What do they look like? What is your sensorial experience of the doors in the corridor?'

'They feel warm,' Sam responded. 'Not hot, but body-temperature. Does this mean someone else has been here before? Is someone else here? Some are warm, some feel like nothing at all.'

'Good, Sam, very good,' Doctor Fahmy said. 'Touch them all.'

Sam wondered if Doctor Fahmy had heard his question and chosen to ignore it. Sam began to touch each of the door knobs in the corridor. He felt perturbed but moved forward, touching the doorknobs After the ninth, he recoiled.

'What just happened, Sam?' Doctor Fahmy asked.

'This doorknob is cold — Very! It sent something like an electric shock through my body,' Sam said. 'Did you see me jump? How did you know something was happening here?'

'Your body is still here in the chair, Sam. You twitched like you'd been having a bad dream,' Doctor Fahmy said.

'Does this happen with your Past Life experiences?' Sam asked.

'Yes, absolutely,' Doctor Fahmy said. 'This is perfectly normal.'

'What should I do now?' Sam asked.

'That's for you to decide. This is all your choosing, Sam, remember? Do you feel that you should walk through the strange door?' Doctor Fahmy asked. 'Or would you like to come back?'

Sam did not respond. He touched the ninth doorknob again. It was cooling this time, almost pleasantly so, now that he knew what to expect.

'Sam?' he heard Doctor Fahmy's voice echo. 'What do you see, Sam? Stay with me.'

'Nothing,' he said.

'Sam,' he heard Doctor Fahmy's voice echo. 'Sam? Sam… Sam!'

And then he had passed the point of hearing Doctor Fahmy's voice.

He walked through the door into the darkness. He felt a sensation like falling, and when it became clear he was still well, falling became like flying — exhilarating. He felt himself in a kind of ecstasy, until he saw a flicker of light waver just before his face once. And then again.

' إيه دہ؟ ' - Ey da?, he heard a voice say - What's this? It was an old woman's voice. A hushed shout. Ambient noise in the background. Howling winds.

Another flicker of light. Then again. A swaying. And then an adroit hand reached into the branches, swaying in the wind and pulled Sam into the spotlight. Sam beheld a pair of eyes, a shadow in a moonlit garden. Sam turned. He had come from a bush. He saw his arm. The old woman's hand protruded from her black cloak and gripped Sam's arm, which was much smaller in circumference than Sam's actual arm, and slightly less hairy.

'Who are you?' the old woman asked. 'Why do you haunt this bush? Go from me, witch!'

Sam inspected the severe and frightened eyes in the cloak for something familiar. He felt overcome with dread. Perhaps this was a nightmare. Sam recalled that is against his faith to communicate with the dead . He was sure there would be some sort of divine retribution for it. Or had his punishment already come to pass? Was this it?

'I know you!' the old woman said. She had been clutching her cloak around her chin. She let it fall open to reveal a striking face like cracking arid earth, lines upon lines around a mouth that had spoken anxious prayers and sorrows for decades. 'Yes, yes — I know you! Although I've never seen your face, I know you... But how?'

Sam said nothing.

'Yes, and I am very happy you have come,' she said, and then grabbing Sam's arm more tightly, entreated him to follow her. Sam felt frightened. He wondered if somewhere in time, in a chaise lounge in Brooklyn, his heart was beating through his chest. He did not know this old woman or her garden, pulling his strange arm to some unknown place.

From the moonlit garden, the old woman pulled Sam

through a passageway — a dark, narrow alley beside a building. He felt a long night shirt dance about his knees. His feet hit the floor with a thud . The old woman, still holding fast to his arm, turned to hush him. 'Easy, easy — But quickly. You mustn't hesitate!' she said in a whisper.

In the alley, Sam wondered about the strange woman. He was conscious that he had neglected to ask Doctor Fahmy what would happen if he were murdered in this alternate reality. There were a great many other questions he realised he had forgotten to address during Doctor Fahmy's long, legally indemnifying preamble.

Beyond the alley was a street with ghostly European edifices, dimly lit by the moonlight and the flickering flames in street lamps. Haussmanian architecture. Stately porticos and windows adorned with relieved marble ornamentations. Sam recognised this as Paris. What then of the unknown Egyptian woman who had whisked him through these streets? She must have had something to do with his family. She had not, after all, been from someplace totally irrelevant like Manhattan or Mongolia. Sam did not recognise her from family photos. She was an old Muslim woman unattached to his family. Sam feared that for all his trouble, he had only arrived at some other family's immigration experience, another exile, another running. Perhaps all of this — including his hypnotherapy session — had been a dream. He had never dreamt in Arabic before.

Finally, the old woman and Sam arrived at a black infinity that knocked the wind out of Sam. Before that infinity was a barren road, then a small sidewalk dotted with street lamps, then another barren road, then a protrusion like a long asphalt bench, then nothing — blackness turning in on itself in waves, like an ocean. The sounds of the wind assaulted his ears. The old woman dragged Sam to the infinity bench and instructed him to sit down.

'What is the meaning of all this?' Sam asked, exasperated. The sound of the wind roared around them. He was afraid the blackness would come and swallow them. 'Doctor Fahmy! What is the meaning of all this?'

'Who are you talking to, child?' the old woman asked, shaking his arm. 'Who is Doctor Fahmy?' Sam couldn't tell her.

'I'm frightened.'

'Frightened? Don't be stupid — Who could be frightened of this? Come.' She reached her black cloak around him like Wassim wrapped Sam in his   טלית - talit - Jewish ritual prayer shawl at their synagogue on Yom Kippur. And there, in the old Muslim woman's cloak, hidden from an unknown infinity of shimmering shadows by another bolt of fabric from another religious observance, tucked under the old Muslim woman's pointed, delicate, little chin, Sam found the strangest thing yet — slumber within a dream.

7. He is Risen Он воскрес

I felt like holding hands with Tony. It was too soon, of course, but we were running out of time. I feared that in the morning, I would regret not having held hands with him, if such things would still matter.

I probably should have been trying to have sex that evening. I think in my situation, a great many men would have started their last night at a gay bar, cruising. But I needed something more significant than I had found in my decade of looking around gay bars. I felt I owed myself something more spectacular even than going out with a bang.

Unusual circumstances sometimes yield improbable and sublime love stories. For example, in *Silence of the Lambs*, following their dialogue at a Tennessee Courthouse, Doctor Hannibal Lecter, imprisoned in a cage at the centre of a room, and Agent Clarice Starling, who is free and interrogating him, touch for the first and last time in the film. At the close of an intense dialogue in which Doctor Lecter finally understands why Agent Starling cares to save a homicidal maniac's victims, Doctor Lecter returns the maniac's case file to Agent Starling through the bars of his cage. Their fingers meet. The camera hones in on that moment's touch. Something unusual happens there. I wouldn't call it sexual or even romantic; I would call it a kind of love. I wanted to gently graze Tony's fingers with mine, like in *Silence of the*

Lambs, a film that stays with you hours later, when you put yourself to bed and turn out the lights. I wanted something exceptional — something to haunt me.

I wondered if I was repeating bad habits — fast and ultimately meaningless expressions of affection that left me feeling more empty than before. I had known enough of that, but I never got used to the disappointment of it. Every time I encountered someone like Tony, I seemed to forget all the life lessons I had learned before. Smarter people grow thick skins. They become good judges of character. I was Sisyphus when it came to matters of the heart; I was born to break, again and again. I had decided that I couldn't allow myself to be broken anymore, because I had no one left to turn to when life went south. No safety net or family to speak of. I was the last of our family, standing on a coast, looking backward.

I put my hands in my pockets. The wind passed through the streets of Brighton Beach like a battalion of spirits. I walked with purpose. Tony matched his pace to mine.

'Where are we off to then?' Tony said with a smile.

'Our first stop is Gastronome No. 46,' I said.

'Gastronome, like gastronomy — More food?' Tony asked.

'Right — a Russian supermarket,' I replied.

'Splendid,' Tony said. I couldn't tell if this was the British sarcasm that is frequently lost on us Americans.

We passed the market's sliding doors. Inside was a hall resembling a Moscow subway station, chandeliers hanging from the ceiling, cream-coloured walls, marble floors, food stations tucked into little nooks. A female attendant stood at a display at the start of the shop with a forest of mushroom-shaped brioche-style breads, topped with white icing and rainbow-coloured sprinkles. A cardboard archway above the attendant's head read Христос воскрес! - Christ is risen! Beside the breads was a basket of hardboiled eggs wrapped in plastic featuring colourful scenes of people in traditional Russian dress tending to farms in the countryside.

My eyes lit up when I beheld the rainbow-sprinkle cakes.

'They're called кулич' - kulich, Tony said.

'You're familiar with Russian food?' I asked.

'Food in general. I run an Instagram foodie account — 46,000 followers, almost,' Tony said. 'I'm a psychologist, though, by trade.'

'Is that why you ended up at Kashkar Cafe?' I asked. 'For Instagram?' I had not recalled him taking food pics, but I was still very high at the restaurant.

'That was the goal, but I didn't get a lot of pics,' Tony said.

He pulled his phone from his brown messenger bag and began to photograph the kulich cakes. The attendant was unamused but said nothing.

'Shall we buy one?' I asked.

'These are like Italian panettone, but a little more festive-looking,' Tony said.

'So they're flavourless and almost always stale,' I said. Tony smiled and rested his eyes on me. I wanted to hold his hand.

We moved through the hall and inspected meats and cheeses, a liquor closet with bottles in Armenian and Georgian script, buckets of all sorts of pickles from cucumbers to tomatoes and lemons, a fish monger with buckets of herring and plates of smoked salmon. Tony stopped on occasion to take photos of the things outsiders might find strange or delightful. The sweets section had a small cooler full of chocolate and vanilla ice creams in red packaging that read only CCCP - Es Es Es Er - USSR. These caught Tony's eye. And then on a shelf beside that was an array of candies with an image of a surprised, blue-eyed child wearing a babushka called Алёнка - Alyonka.

Finally we arrived at a self-service buffet. We inspected the offerings with wonderment —

плов - plov - Central Asian pilaff with meat and carrots

котлетки - kotlietki - chicken cutlets

Шуба - shuba. The sign in English read 'Herring in Fur Coat.' Strata of what appeared to be beets, some other vegetables, and of course the herring, swaddled like several more salads at the bar in a coat of glossy mayonnaise. Tony took a close-up shot of Herring in a Fur Coat so close that he had to wipe the mayonnaise from his mobile camera lens. He showed me the photo. It looked like an infrared shot of Mars, seen from above.

'I of course have no qualified opinions on food, beyond being a curious human who eats — I just take pictures of unusual dishes and put filters on them. But of all the cuisines I take pics of, I'm especially impressed by Russian food,' Tony said.

'Impressed?'

Tony ladled a hunk of Herring in Fur Coat and then allowing it to plop back down into itself with a jiggle buoyed by mayonnaise. 'What's awful about it is what impresses me,' he said. Look at these dishes. They have all the ingredients of universally loved comfort foods: Heaps of oil, potatoes, meat, cream. And they're still horrible. It must take great skill to make such awful food from good ingredients.'

I offered Tony a smile signifying amusement.

'You know what also impresses me?' Tony asked. 'You. That you love it here.'

'Don't you also love it here?' I asked. 'The herring in a coat is straight out of Doctor Seuss.'

'How often do you come here?' Tony asked.

'Often!' I said, avoiding his gaze in a tray of beef stroganoff. There was a small dish of sliced lemons on the side. I reckoned it validated Tony's view of Russian cuisine that Gastronome No. 46 should encourage its customers to curdle the stroganoff's cream with lemon.

'Once a month?' Tony asked. I looked into his eyes, smiled as an indication to him that there would be no answer, and moved on along the buffet line, inspecting the other offerings.

'Weekly?' Tony asked, following me. My smile had been lost in translation.

'Sometimes more than once in a week, depending on my mood,' I said.

'Are you very into Russia — or the former Soviet Union or Uyghur dumplings?' Tony asked.

'Not especially. I'll have to give it more thought, when I've got the time. I don't usually like to interrogate myself in this way,' I said. That was a lie. My whole life had been a self-interrogation. But Tony's line of questioning made me uneasy, and I needed him to shut up. His questions were beginning to plunge me into myself. For this reason — and my family's cultural distaste for analysis and the examined life — I had never been to a shrink. We were certain that particularly in a hyper-capitalist society, the function of therapy is to drown people deeper into their wayward thoughts to make a buck. I looked at Tony, the psychologist, out of the side of my eye as we continued along the buffet. He was, save his benign, little food pictures and his charming demeanour, part of a system designed to drown uneasy, vulnerable people in manageable sorrows that become psychosis.

Back on the street, strolling with Tony away from Gastronome No. 46, I found myself deep in thought. I noticed a gift shop called Kalinka Gifts had an image of what appeared to be a stock art smiling man holding a wrapped package. Below him was a tagline reading, 'Life is a gift.' Beside the shop, just under the subway overpass, a woman with an oddly familiar face leaned against the wall. She was rotund, with a short, bouffant hairdo. She wore a tight black and grey Justin Bieber shirt — probably from one of the Brighton discount clothing shops — and a short, frilly, rainbow-coloured skirt. Knock-off slip-on Vans. She looked up at the train passing loudly overhead. She took a drag off of a long, thin lady cigarette.

I recalled that I too had been a smoker. I had almost forgotten. I felt for a moment that I could easily become a smoker again. I could almost feel a cigarette between my index and middle fingers. Perhaps in some other corner of the multiverse, I was still a smoker. *Was I happy there? Or was I asphyxiated and hastening towards death?* No, matter, I thought — I wanted to see the hot air expel from my chest and disappear. And then, amid my thoughts of smoking, I yawned and the thoughts went away. It was that easy. A yawn. Like magic.

From the corner of my eye, I noticed Tony looking at me, inspecting me with great intensity. What had I done wrong?

I realised I had neglected to cover my mouth and did so a moment too late.

'Sorry,' I said. Tony said nothing at all. Unnerving.

The wind travelled from the ocean through the long corridors of Brighton Beach's side streets, past apartment buildings that resembled austere Soviet housing blocks. The old women and men who lived in those buildings spent their days and evenings sitting outside of their buildings, perched on the makeshift chair flaps on the back of their walkers, which they all got from the same medical supply store on Brighton Beach Avenue. They kept guard like the sullen gargoyles of Notre Dame, engaging the younger passersby in mostly unwanted conversation. The disintegrating Soviet gargoyles of Brighton Beach, wistful for an era where everyone knew and cared for their neighbours — or alternatively informed on them — sat unfazed in the winds, which came in from the Atlantic Ocean like a 1950s invisible movie monster. But for me, the intermittent howling crept into my mind and joined my thoughts to my strange love for Brighton Beach. Perhaps the sorrowful howling of the Atlantic was why I had loved Brighton Beach.

I wondered if Brighton Beach and my strange love for it would be the same in the morning. I wondered if whether I loved Brighton or not would still matter.

8. Lighthouses منارات

The legendary Lighthouse of Alexandria is older than the so-called Common Era.

It was one of the wonders of the so-called ancient world, destroyed in a series of earthquakes in the 14th century. The Alexandrians — the ones who remain in Alexandria — still cling to it today. By 'today,' I mean that they cling to it as late as the 21st century. The Lighthouse and not the equally legendary Library of Alexandria — which still exists not in its original building, but as a functioning institution of the city — is the modern-day, 21st Century Alexandria University emblem. That is a curious thing indeed, since one might assume that a historically significant library would be a more fitting emblem for a university. But then, the Arabic root of the word for lighthouse, منور , means brilliant and illuminating in the same literal and figurative senses as their English translations.

A great many powerful minds attend that university — the future leaders of the country. They wear shirts and sweatshirts with school emblems bearing testament to a building erected and felled long before our elders were born. Shards of the Lighthouse are said to be built into another of Egypt's great, mournful monuments to hallowed dead things, the Citadel of Qaitbay. It is unsurprising to me that a long-gone Lighthouse continues to haunt living and breathing Egyptians today. It is unsurprising, because I am constitutionally like Egypt, my great familiar unknown: I am prone to hold too tightly to dead things.

I am like Egypt in other respects. For instance, in 2011, I too was in a state of movement. I graduated from journalism school with a job as a rookie reporter at the United Nations bureau of الحوار - El Hiwar, which you may know to be an Arab media with a global footprint, with multilingual broadcasts both in the Arab region and in the so-called West. Just after the uprisings, I was in Tamazgha, the North African nation cobbled together by the departing French from several of our nations. I reported the immediate aftermath of the mass-movement — constitutional reform and the building up of institutions for government accountability. I wrote articles in English for the Hiwar website. My boss back at the New York bureau had arranged for me to spend a month in Tamazgha. I rented an apartment in the capital city of Matoubia. That was where I met him.

He was like the night, hair like the unshorn wool of a black lamb. Quiet. I remember him now, only as the light from the lighthouses on the Tamazghan coast splashed across part of his face. Call him Omri. I won't speak his real name, for fear that someone will learn it and use what we had to stop his work for our people's lives and dignity.

Omri and I were sitting in the back seat of a speeding vehicle. Omri and his friends were government accountability activists. Activists are *militants*, in French, which they often spoke in tandem with their native Arabic. Growing up in the U.S., it struck me as interesting that the word for activist in

51

French has such violent connotations in English — militant. But I never asked anyone whether the word was similarly aggressive in French, because when you are a journalist — a generalist, writing about everything under the sun — you need to learn fast and rarely admit to the magnitude of your ignorance. Journalism was always an ill-fitting profession, for me. I enjoyed not knowing in that car. I enjoyed that I could only see the salient bits of Omri — his mouth, his hand discreetly reaching for mine, illuminated by the lighthouses on the coast. It was not the actual lighthouse light, to be accurate — It was champagne-coloured flood lights illuminating the lighthouses as regal reminders of Tamazgha's long history of maritime trade. It was there for the foreign dignitaries who were among the nation's helms people and the tourists who stayed at beachside resorts outside of the nation's capital — resorts emptied by the tumult of the time. Today, the seaside resorts are still crammed with sunbathing foreigners who have no idea or interest in what life is like for people living in shantytowns only a few kilometres away.

In the front passenger's seat was Nawel, an interview source who had turned into a friend. She was a poet who had taken to the streets, responding to calls from Tunisia and then from Egypt. Her words in our interviews had enchanted me. She lived life as thought she were an extended metaphor from one of her poems. Every gesture was pregnant with meaning. She was a manifestation of indignation, of popular will, and of humanity. She was hard. No one's fool. Nawel introduced me to Omri at Café Les Phares, the late-night watering hole in downtown Matoubia where they convened with their comrades after rallies at the Tamazghan Parliament, blocks away.

'He's a bisexual,' she confided just before Omri joined us. When he arrived, his eyes set on me like a swarm of locusts. I became a performance artist, in his eyes. Every time I lifted a cigarette to my mouth, his gaze followed my forearm to-and-fro. In the alchemy of his eyes, I became conscious of my limbs and the ballet bras croisé he had found there. The little flame of my lighter illuminated my face. Fire felt unusually warm. My life had all of a sudden become more remarkable, in his experience of it.

Together, the three of us hopped on trains and traveled the country. I reported. They made contact with likeminded people. At the end of the day, in hostels and spare bedrooms, we smoked and chatted into the small hours of the morning, Nawel regaling us with her poetry until the hostel night staff told her to leave the men's floor.

Monsef was an art professor and part of their circle. We encountered him at Les Phares before a night out on the town, in bars and underground dance halls with windows boarded up with planks and cardboard. After a festive night, Monsef — who had a car and was therefore popular with his friends — drove us to a late-night eatery. He took the scenic route, along the coast. He blasted اهواك - Ahwak, the love song by the long-dead so-called Brown Nightingale, Abdel Halim Hafez. Hafez was from Egypt, the homeland thousands of kilometres from Tamazgha that I had stayed away from since my fool's departure, years before.

At the very moment Monsef played a much loved, classic Egyptian song in my honour, I was making Egypt impossible for myself. Unwittingly. No one knew what I was doing at that very moment, just by having a journalism job — not in our car in Tamazgha or in Egypt, thousands of miles away.

At the restaurant, we gathered around a large plate of salads surrounding fries and chicken stuffed with parsley and rice. There was a photo of the interim prime minister hanging parallel to some stock art of a rotisserie chicken. I reckon that the thinly veiled insult to the authorities was precisely why they chose this place.

Nawel and Monsef filled their mouths with chicken and discussions about the nation's overwhelming and uncertain future. They spoke as if they would one day compete for office. I wasn't paying attention. Omri's hand caressed my knee under the table once and then again. Little flashes of light.

'The project of a free Tamazgha lives at night!' Monsef declared to the table, rousing me from my reverie of chicken and romance. I had not been listening to the conversation that preceded it. Then Monsef excused himself to the washroom.

'So beautiful!' I proclaimed.

Nawel, who had been sitting close to me, leaned in and spoke in a whisper. 'The project of a free Tamazgha could live in the daylight too, if he had any guts,' she said. Her eyes penetrated mine.

Months later, I was back in New York. Nawel messaged me on Facebook to confess that she and Omri had been in a relationship since I left Matoubia. She said that Omri frequently expressed guilt about what he had told her was a treason against me and that he wanted my blessing. *Write us a little note*, Nawel wrote. *It would mean a lot to us.*

In the final scene of *Jules & Jim*, the French New Wave picture, Catherine lightheartedly entreats Jules to watch her before she drives Jim and herself off a bridge to their deaths. I felt I had the opportunity to be Marian in my compassion and spiritual generosity. But then, there was also room for some gentle cruelty.

I emailed Tamazgha.

Dear Nawel and Omri,

Life is hard, so I'm happy you have each other. Go fuck yourselves.

Ma3 L7ob

S

As my luck would have it, this was not the first or last man I had been intimate with who ended up with a woman. It feels by now like my lot in life to drive men to heterosexuality. That is, the men who want more than just sex, since I don't know what happens to the many others who only want casual hookups. Maybe they also turn to women. Maybe my feeling that I scare my lovers straight is a Baader-Meinhoff phenomenon type-situation — a frequency illusion — a false sense that when it rains it pours — a misbelief that random occurrences are connected parts of a grand design. Or maybe something about me is indeed so difficult that I seem to turn my dudes away from the whole male gender. Or maybe it's just the opposite. Maybe my love is so powerful that I ruin men in the way Jimi Hendrix smashed his guitars. The latter idea makes me smile.

In Omri's defence, I know that when I left Matoubia, I had no intention of ever returning for him.

9. The House on Flower Street

دارنا بشارع الزهرة

Sam discovered that Wassim's eyes had become smaller with old age. Wassim used to blame his spectacles for this, Sam recalled. By contrast, the eyes of the younger man sitting before Sam at a heavy wooden dining room table with gold-plated embellishments were remarkably larger. As a teenager, Wassim had the eyes of Ancient Egyptian frescoes — eyes the shape of enormous almonds, with a straight horizontal line of black running out toward the ears, like stems. Some Americans dressing as Ancient Egyptians for Halloween costume parties draw this line with eyeliner, to look as Wassim and his family had as a birthright. The young Wassim's eyes were fixed on his grandson.

A young woman woke Sam and the old Muslim woman who held him in her cloak with a shout.

'Whatever are you doing out here with this stranger, Heaven help us!' the young woman shouted. Sam observed the young woman. She had a thick profusion of heat-straightened black hair tied tightly behind her head. Sam imagined that her pinched expression was soured by the tightness of her up-do. She wore a cream-coloured frock that was synched tightly at the waist with an ebony belt. Sam's first impression of her was to wonder if this woman ever indulged in an excess of food. Then he wondered how she breathed.

The young woman reached for the old woman's arm.

Startled awake, the old woman gathered her faculties and swatted the young woman away.

'I don't owe you explanations, girl. You must be insane to talk to me that way ,' the old woman said.

'I must be!' the young woman exclaimed with a guffaw. 'You're making us all crazy, wandering town doing Heaven knows what. Come now. Time to come home. Say goodbye to your friend.'

While the young and old women argued, Sam surveyed what had been the shimmering expanse of nothingness from the night before. In the early morning sunlight, crisp and blindingly bright, he recognised this place. He knew it well from so many black-and-white photos on Instagram. It was not Paris or the majestic and overwhelming black infinity he had seen the night before, but something else altogether. It was the Alexandria corniche. The clouds hung so low over the water that he felt he could reach up and run his fingers through them as they sped along. Fisherman swayed on the waves in rowboats. On the large avenue behind them, Sam heard the sound of a mule-drawn carriage passing and the occasional automobile sputtering along, engines roaring. Alexandria was grand, Sam thought — larger than he had anticipated it would be, even as immense as Cairo had seemed in his botched return so many years before — or rather, decades later. Transfixed, Sam leapt up and almost floated away along the corniche. The old woman shouted after him.

'Come back here— you,' she said. 'Remind me of your name, child. I'm old.'

'Sam,' he replied, half-awake and half-engrossed by the

time and place. Not much had changed, he remarked; the buildings looked more or less as they had in the 21st century photos of Alexandria on Instagram, but here, the polish and lustre of youth was still with them. So too were the saturated colours that had faded and chipped with time. On the opposite side of the road from the corniche were large European-style edifices. There was a park in the distance with some palm trees. Beyond the buildings in the immediate vicinity was what appeared to be a large minaret. Up the coast was a great square with people rushing to work. A farmer passed behind them on the sidewalk with a large, rusty wheelbarrow full of produce, shouting to would-be customers to come purchase what he billed as the very last of the oranges. 'Time is running out! The oranges are leaving. Bid them farewell!' he cried.

'Sama, come here,' the old woman told Sam.

Sam noticed that the passersby seemed offended by him. Two women strolling along the waterfront, their arms linked in a sweet way that would become rare, observed Sam with visible disapproval. A man rushing past held his fedora to his head to keep the sea from carrying it off on a gust of wind. The man glared at the scene transpiring on the asphalt barrier beside the Alexandria waterfront.

'Please, please let's take this inside before someone calls the police,' the young woman pleaded from between her teeth, lowering her gaze and her voice in embarrassment.

Sam inspected the young woman closely. She had to have been a relative of his. He had seen her face before, in old photos. Beside her was a young man, silent and perplexed, who looked at Sam. Sam had waited for so long to meet

58

Wassim again. Sam did not dare to ask himself if this was the young Wassim. Sam looked away. He feared that if he allowed himself to look at the young Wassim, so beautiful and full of life and colour like the buildings that surrounded him, Sam would cry, which he knew to be a great shame for the Saadoun family, particularly the men.

'This is not a stranger — I know Sama,' the old woman said, wrapping her cloak around Sam's shoulders. *Who the fuck is Sama?* Sam wondered.

On their way back to the house, Sam was transfixed by a number of shops bearing the name of his family's street — Flower Street. There was a dressmaker, a florist, and a small restaurant, tucked between great mansions that were nothing like the shadows he had seen in the lamplight the night before. All announced that they were on Flower Street, in signs painted above their shop windows and doors in creamsicle-oranges and pomegranate-reds. The old Muslim woman held tightly to Sam under her cloak, covering the two of them and pulling Sam along. Sam felt frustrated. He would have liked to buy a souvenir from this street. He worried that at any moment he could slip out of his hypnotic state, and he would have nothing to show for a night's homelessness in 1930s Alexandria but an ethereal, hazy moment. Then he realised the folly of his consumerism and that souvenirs likely don't travel well along the brainwaves or the time-space continuum, or whatever this journey had been. Whatever he purchased in Alexandria would stay in Alexandria.

Sam felt an unusual heaviness in his chest, as they walked up Flower Street. He thought it was the overwhelming emotion of that moment. But then he put his hand to his chest and found there, beneath his long night shirt, a more superficial weight: two small breasts. He felt dizzy and then amazed by two little bits of flesh, no heavier than the oranges the farmworker sold by the kilo on the corniche.

'What does this mean, Doctor Fahmy?' Sam said under his breath, flummoxed by his figure.

No answer came. Sam wondered if Doctor Fahmy had abandoned him — if all of this was transpiring in the space of time it took for her to make herself a cup of tea in the kitchen beside her pantry-office in 21st century Brooklyn. Perhaps hypnosis was just as she had described it: a solo act.

'Do you see how she's dressed, Wassim?' Sam overheard the young woman whisper to the young man, confirming that he was Sam's grandfather. Sam recognised the young, nervous woman as his great aunt Lilia. 'Now we're bringing who knows what kind of people into our home, Heaven help us. Poor baba will be very upset,' Lilia said.

Sam — or rather Sam(a), forgive me — was greeted by the familiar, pungent smell of بخور - boukhour - Arab incense burning in a small censer in the corner of the foyer at the entrance of the house on Flower Street.

First Lilia invited Sam(a) up a flight of stairs leading from the foyer to the room she shared with her sister Ghozala. There, Lilia retrieved a teal frock and sapphire belt for Sam(a) and left her to change. Sam(a) surveyed her naked self in a full-length mirror and decided — with little frame of reference — that she had a lovely body. Sam's absence of muscle had translated into something much more appealing as a woman than she could have ever hoped to be as a man. Changing in the mirror, Sam(a) was almost shocked by how beautiful she had become. She left the belt behind in Lilia and Ghozala's room.

To Sam(a)'s knowledge, Sam had been a man in his waking life. But Sam(a) had to have come from somewhere, she thought. Like this whole hypnotherapy session, Sam(a) was unsure whether her gender in 1930s Alexandria was external or internal — whether this was a kind of Wizard of Oz voyage to another dimension, or if all of these people and sights existed in her own reckoning of things. If they had only existed in her mind, Sam(a) wondered, did that mean that she had always been a woman? Was this a manifestation of something buried deep inside? Wouldn't she have known? Sam had acknowledged he was gay — Sam had been out for more than a decade. She recalled though that when she came out, she had been relieved not to be trans— She had been relieved to be a sort of Queer that she could ignore and then, when that became impossible, that she could hide. Her Queerness had never demanded that she announce it physically, except for in the sort of intimacy Sam would never have discussed with his parents, even if he were straight.

The old Muslim woman sat next to Sam(a) at the large dining room table. The room was adorned on one wall with a fresco of some flowers and ribbon. A small chandelier hung from the ceiling, and behind Wassim was a hutch full of fine china and glassware.

Sam(a) was surprised that the old woman was not among the family's help staff — that she joined them to eat at the dining room table. Wassim's sister Lilia, who had escorted Sam(a) inside, was in the kitchen beside the dining room, preparing ful medammes for the family. The boiling brine-cured fava beans, peeled hardboiled eggs, and Arab bread warming on the stovetop perfumed the dining room, overpowering the incense creeping in from the hall. Lilia spoke mostly inaudible, frantic words with her sister Ghozala in between bringing dishes and fixings like olive oil and lemon wedges to the table. 'What will we tell baba when he comes home?' Sam(a) heard one of her great aunts say.

Whenever Ghozala — who would become Giselle when the family moved to London and then to the U.S. — approached the table, she offered Sam(a) a little smile. Like Lilia, she died when Sam(a) was very young. Sam(a) did not know her. And yet, there was a flicker of sharpness and beauty in her eyes. Sam(a) wondered if somewhere inside, she too was excited to have more family. Ghozala was a woman with round features: animated circles and ovals with some shading. She had the appearance of a real, full-fledged person with skin and hair and nails, but energetically, to Sam(a)'s mind, Ghozala was as a half-finished drawing of a woman. A nose, a mouth. A smile. A feeling. A ghost. Sam(a) felt frightened, and then, as most children acclimate to the fearful dark, she grew accustomed to what was frighting about the ghosts moving between the dining room and the kitchen.

Wassim stared at Sam(a). Sam(a) could not meet his gaze. But from the periphery of Sam(a)'s vision, she saw her young grandfather staring at her, his left eye squinting in the way the old Wassim's left eye would when he was deep in thought. Sam(a) wondered if somewhere in the universe of Wassim's mind, he knew she was his grandson.

'He knows!' shouted the old Muslim woman, who had been resting her eyes on the wall before her. The exclamation startled Sam(a), who looked at the old Muslim woman, speechless. Everyone else ignored the old Muslim woman entirely. *Were these the rules of this dimension? The old Muslim woman can read thoughts? And if this had been time travel and not just a product of something in Sam(a)'s mind, was 1930s Alexandria magic? Were there soothsayers in the time-before land? Where then were the belly dancers and snake-charmers?* Sam(a) wondered if there had always been a latent Orientalism to her reckoning of this home, buried deep inside, beneath a veneer of self-respect.

The sisters sat down to breakfast. Sam(a) watched the old Muslim woman break off pieces of Arab bread, crush the ful medammes with egg, lemon, and olive oil, and bring it to her small, wizened mouth, the crown of wrinkles adorning it dancing in unison as she chewed heartily. Her face, once a shadow in a cloak, was becoming more familiar to Sam(a) now. She had survived times of want and epidemics. She tasted food.

'Look closely. Somewhere in their eyes, they all know,' the old Muslim woman told Sam(a) before scooping up another bit of ful. No one looked up from their plates when she said this. Sam(a) wondered if they could hear her at all, in 1930s Alexandria.

10. Kalinka Кали́нка

Tony sat beside me at a small table, eyes drilling into me. We were waiting for the show to start. I sighed deeply.

'There it is!' Tony exclaimed. I looked at him. He was sitting too close for my comfort. I could feel his warm breath cutting through the ocean air, drifting into our boardwalk restaurant from the shore.

'There's something in the way you sigh,' he continued. 'Like before, by the subway overpass, you seemed to yawn or something — so deeply, it made me feel like I myself was suffocating. It wasn't just breathing. It was as though—'

A waiter arrived with our vodka shots. Thankfully.

'To your health, Tony!' I said, heartily, truncating the conversation. *Maybe now you can stop policing my breath*, I thought, politely smiling as I lifted the little glass, frosted and holding a dram of premium Russian vodka. As it traveled down my throat, I tasted none of the rubbing alcohol flavour of inferior brands — just a hint of toasted walnut , warm and smooth.

The restaurant was crowded for the first show of the evening. A trio of men sat at a large round table just in front of Tony and I, their faces rouged with drink and puckered with the pickles they ate as chasers. One of the men was relatively thin and emotionless, observing the other two, physically larger and more animated, exchanging jovial shouts and belly laughs. Ignoring Tony, I watched the quiet, thin man, who held an unlit cigarette between his thumb and index finger. The lights dimmed, and a master of ceremonies made an announcement in Russian over the loudspeaker. The thin man excused himself and bolted to the boardwalk just beyond the restaurant to smoke his cigarette. The faint smell crept indoors from where the quiet, thin man stood. It crept into my nose.

Over a few loudspeakers in the corners of the room came a crescendo that ended with a bang. The audience sat in the darkness, rapt in silence. Then the music began as a whisper — 'Калинка, калинка, калинка моя' - Kalinka, kalinka, kalinka maya. Strobe lights illuminated five men dressed in brown wool Red Army soldier costumes. As the song escalated into complete frenzy, they performed a Kozachok, each dancer offering a solo comprised of a variation of the squat dance.

Kalinka. I thought on the souvenir shop we had passed named Kalinka, probably after this song. I thought on the shop's stock-art smiling man, and its tagline: *Life is a gift.* I don't know that I agree. The more I see of life, the less certain I am of what it is. A separation, maybe.

I sighed deeply, and then that sigh turned into a yawn, which turned into a gasp. Easy as that—whatever tightness I had felt in my chest had gone. I hadn't even noticed the tightness — the strange desire I had once before — until it left my chest. Like magic. I was uncertain whether this remarkable effect was an act of the occult or a function of my strange subconscious, but what did it matter? I was free.

Tony startled me when he slammed his hand on mine with the gusto of the music pounding in our ears. I turned to find him staring at me. I wondered if he had seen any of the show, or if his face had been fixed on mine the whole time. I could smell the walnut scent of the vodka, like a beautiful perfume, emerging from his mouth onto my cheek. His face was illuminated with the ruby red of the stage lights, bleeding into the crowd. It evened his complexion.

'That's it,' he said. I read his lips — I could not hear him past *Kalinka*. 'The yawn.'

I turned back to the show. I had no response for Tony. He slipped his fingers through mine and tightened his grasp, and in an instant, I had forgotten the anxiety from before. His hand had been like a weighted blanket on me. I could have slept right there, as though the thunderous *Kalinka* of the Red Army Choir playing on the restaurant sound system had been a little lullaby.

One of the larger men at the table in front of us had been unabashedly fixing his gaze on our interwoven hands. He then looked into our faces and shot us a disapproving look. We remained there for a moment, suspended in his condemnation, until he looked away. Our hands parted. A moment later, we settled the tab and continued to make our way down Brighton Beach. We had to make haste, I told Tony, before gesturing to a waiter for the bill. We had very little time left before everything in Brighton would close for the night.

11. Egyptian, Modern

Once — that is, just weeks before that night in Brighton — there was a young modern-day man in Alexandria called Akram who wanted to pull my cultural references out of the 1930s, into the present. Akram was a law student in his early 20s. He had an Instagram account.

In the 21st century, Akram was youthful, like my grandfather Wassim had been in the 20th. Nearly a century apart, both were in their times, of the same class of young men known in Alexandria as the شباب - shabab - the dudes. I was never one of the shabab and never would be. I have come to respect — despite myself — that there are understandings Akram and Wassim will share that I will never fathom. That is not only a function of my gayness or my femininity or my never having seen Alexandria but from just beyond its city gate; it is also because they both had the privilege of being raised by young people.

I came to Akram in the same roundabout way I ended up back in Alexandria in the 30s. Years after I returned to New York, I left my job at Hiwar, the international Arab news outlet. As with Egypt, the sense of frenzied movement there had been in 2011 seemed only a few years later to calcify in me until it became something cynical. I stopped reporting my own stories. I became a freelance editor, dolling up other people's thoughts, and to fulfil the creative need in me, I wrote a book about Wassim, cobbled together from ideas of what his life could mean to the world — a journalistic interrogation of his existence, the history surrounding it, and a political theory emanating from and applied to it. Akram had read another incarnation of himself in the book about Wassim — a sort of time-travel that set him on the course of concocting his own theories. That was why he reached out. He wanted to tell me that like me, he saw some of Wassim everyday, in the mirror.

I had a knack for disappearing myself, at the time. In the book, I was as the negative space in a stencilled rendering of the man who raised me. When the book caused a bit of a fuss with some trolls — nothing unexpected, but exhausting all the same — I wiped the internet clean of my email address. The only remaining way to reach out was the Instagram Direct Message requests, which I had the habit of summarily deleting.

But as luck would have it, one night, asphyxiated by the all-consuming dark solitude in my Lower East Side studio, I read Akram's message request. He had responded to a post — a photo of the Oum Kalthoum monument in Cairo's Zamalek neighbourhood. In the caption I wrote: 'You can't go home again.' No hashtags. No comments allowed.

Akram: ليش كده يا سامي؟ *(- Leish kida ya Sami - Oh Sam, why so?)*

> Me: *Why can't I go home again? It's the title of an American book. I felt it was fitting.*

But why this title and a photo of Cairo?

Does the caption upset you? Because I don't have the energy to navigate your emotions

Not at all bro — just asking a question!

You don't have to answer of course

But maybe you should come home again!

You say that like you're calling me home for dinner. Come to dinner, Sam, why not? My mum will make you a molokheya so good that you won't leave.

Thank you and your mom! But it's not so easy.

Isn't it?

No.

Why? Because you are Jewish? There are many Egyptian people with Jewish origins still living in Egypt.

No, that's not it.

Because you are gay then?

...

How do you know that? I didn't talk about it in the book...

Just a hunch — I Googled your journalism, and you've reported some stories on gay issues. There are many gay people in Egypt. I have a lesbian friend.

Ah ok. No, it's neither of those things. I was a gay and Jewish Egyptian person the first and last time I went back to Egypt.

What is it then?

You'd laugh if I told you, and that laughter might hurt me, so let's forget it.

Try me. I'm not an internet troll. I don't know why you expect me to be cruel

Fair enough.

Before I wrote the book, I was a reporter for El Hiwar, which is banned there now, as you may know.

Right, for pushing the Brotherhood.

Right. On the Arabic site, from what I'm told, since I don't have good enough Arabic to read Arabic news. On the English-language end, we were just doing journalism. Or the folks I knew on my level did. Reported stories out, verified them, no political axe to grind...

Anyway, I have no opinion on the matter of Hiwar, the Brotherhood, any of it. I have no thought or motive other than hoping Egyptian people live with dignity. And I was at the very bottom of the corporate totem pole there, reporting little Web stories. But my former colleagues have told me it could be dangerous if a border control person decided to Google my name at the airport or something. Meanwhile, I'm just a man who was standing in the wrong place at the wrong time, professionally.

I see — Yes, a difficult situation. Nothing funny about that.

Isn't it, though? Overnight, it seemed that because I took a job in a dying industry in my 20s, I was branded an Islamist threat. A gay Jewish Egyptian Islamist threat.

I suppose that's a little funny.

Ironically, it reminds me of the premise of the Egyptian Movie Kebab and Terrorism with Adel Imam.

Yes! The unwitting terrorist!

Where they force an innocent man suspected of terrorism to make demands, and he requests the delivery of tons of kebab.

This does have the flavour of Adel Imam humour.

So you know Adel Imam. Your family left in the 1940s and 50s, but you still got Egyptian movies in America.

At Arab goods shops here in the U.S.

Anyway, I'll never see the House on Flower Street from my book, because I left Cairo in haste.

You left Egypt in haste, like the Passover saying. I remember that from the book. Your Exodus.

Right. I tried to see Flower Street on Google maps. There are no street-level views of it.

Why didn't you continue on to Alexandria when you had the chance? That part, I didn't understand in the book.

I wouldn't write about that sort of thing in a book about my parents, but I had a nervous breakdown in Cairo. I couldn't stay. I wouldn't have emerged from the big, dark void I was in.

I'm sorry.

Nothing for you to be sorry about. Only me.

The next day, Akram sent me a link to a Spotify playlist with exactly five hours, fifty-five minutes of Egyptian hip hop and hipstery alt-rock songs. An introduction to our new bards.

Hey bro.

Thought I'd send you this to update your cultural references, he wrote. Gotta run, TTYL.

The title of the Spotify playlist was *Egyptian, Modern.* Listening to it, I found myself moved by the poetry of our young people. For days, I listened to it on repeat, imagining what my life would be like on the tram to and from work, in Alexandria in the 21st century. I reckoned I would have a wife and kids and go to Shabbat services every Friday. Maybe I would recognise my attraction to men late enough in my life for my sexual orientation not to matter at all.

On that tram around an Alexandria of the mind, I thought about how a child had sent me a list of music to make me *Egyptian, Modern.* Had history panned out differently — had the world allowed us to stay, and had I still somehow been born, I would have introduced these songs to him, in some contemporary Egyptian culture or poetry or music course that I would teach at some highbrow Egyptian school like the American University of Cairo. Or perhaps, in that other reality, I would have been musically talented myself. I would have been a modern-day Mohammed Abdel Wahab, or some such singer-songwriter-phenomenon-of-song.

My minor frustration with being schooled by a child raised some questions about life that can yield no answer. But they were not rhetorical questions, surely, since they were a great deal weightier than rhetoric: *At what point would I become a full-fledged person, for where we're from? Was I a full-fledged person in the so-called West? Or would I always be a child of our children, understanding only a faint tea of things?*

Worse yet, was I a stillborn?

12. To the Moon إلى القمر

Cake for breakfast, Sam(a) thought. *Alexandria in the 30s is paradise.*

The family had finished breakfast and their father had not yet returned to behold the stranger in their home.

'I have just the thing!' proclaimed Lilia, panicked as she had been since Sam(a) first met her on the corniche. Lilia emerged from the kitchen with a chocolate cake, topped with dollops of apricot jam and roasted pecans. Lilia delicately served Sam(a) a thin slice on a plate decorated with a scene of the European imagination of a Chinese palatial pagoda and the high-born ladies of some imperial court in flowing tunics and shawls. Already sufficiently full from the ful medammes, Sam(a) very quickly devoured the cake and asked for a second slice. Lilia was happy to oblige.

'This is the most spectacular cake I've eaten in any time or place!' Sam(a) declared. This was a mental manipulation. From her grandfather's stories of Lilia, Sam(a) knew Lilia to be this way — a perpetually anxious person whose benchmark for self-worth was cake. Sam(a) noticed a look of appeasement wash over Lilia's face before she looked down in Marian grace.

'Enjoy it,' Wassim said. 'She won't let us have any.' These were the first words he had spoken to Sam(a). His voice sounded crisp and pure, Sam(a) thought, recalling that

Wassim would become a smoker in New York. Until he died, he would open the kitchen window in their flat and have a cigarette with his morning coffee. Tears emerged from Sam(a)'s eyes. It had been so long since she had heard the old man voice that this would become.

'It's for guests — my speciality,' Lilia said with a gracious smile. Lilia then shot Wassim a scornful grimace. And then, beholding Sam(a)'s tears salting her cake, Lilia asked, 'Why are you crying, darling Sama? Is something the matter?'

Sam(a) shook her head, as she searched her mind for something to say. 'Not at all! It's been so long since I've tasted something so nice.'

Lilia reached into the pocket of her cream-coloured frock and produced a scarlet handkerchief that she used to dab Sam(a)'s tears. The old Muslim woman put her strong, arthritic hand on Sam(a)'s back and sturdily patted it. And then the old Muslim woman began to groan as though she would produce some magic gem from her mouth.

'Br,' she effected, with a deflation of her chest.

'What's that?' Lilia said, a look of panic returning to her face.

'Br..brrrr,' the Old Muslim Woman said.

'What are you trying to say?' asked Ghozala, who had been silently watching the exchange, smiling strangely.

'Brrrrrookli!' the Old Muslim Woman declared. 'Brookli?' she asked, finding herself confusing.

Sam(a) looked at the old Muslim woman, mouth agape. Her expression of shock turned to a smile, as the old Muslim woman kept trying to form a sensical word. 'Brikoloun, brooklouna.'

'You'll have to excuse our grandmother. Her mind gets away from her — like her feet,' Wassim said. Wassim's sisters smiled.

'Your grandmother?' Sam(a) asked, with some shock.

'Yes, she lives with our grandfather in the small flat we built for them in our garden,' Lilia said. 'They are from another time — dress from another time, think from another time.'

'Tfou on you all!' said the grandmother, whom Sam(a) recalled just barely was named Hawa — Hava in the Hebrew for the prayers Sam(a) and Wassim would say to mourn this face that Sam(a) had never seen.

'Donkey children,' Hawa continued. This comment set them all, except Sam(a) who was still dazed by the circumstances, into laughter. Hawa also laughed, but where the children found the insult humorous, Hawa laughed at her arrogant, cultureless donkey children.

Hawa stopped laughing suddenly. 'Over the moon!' she proclaimed with great conviction and seriousness. Another ejection from somewhere inside her.

'What does it mean?' an amused Ghozala asked Hawa. 'What is there over the moon, grandma?'

'I don't know, my dear, but I had to say it,' Hawa said, visibly perplexed. 'Barkawi. Over the moon. Maybe they are thoughts from Heaven, who knows?' And with that, Hawa the great-great-grandmother took Sam(a)'s hand and squeezed it tightly. She had a great force in her hands, despite the arthritis that contorted them.

There were no photos of Sam(a)'s great-great-grandmother Hawa in their home in New York. There was a single portrait of her husband, Adam, in a gilded frame. Sam(a) had always

76

wondered why there were no photos of Hawa. Sam(a) looked into her face. Her skin was like clay soil, cracked and brown. Too many lines to count. Black hair, tied back under her cloak. A strong nose.

'I have also thirsted to see your face, Sama,' Hawa said. 'What a great miracle, thank Heaven, that I should see it in this lifetime!'

Out of view, Sam(a) heard a door open. Lilia shot Wassim and Ghozala a look. Sam(a)'s heart sank. Hawa was unconcerned with her son's arrival. Her mental calculus was planted firmly over the moon.

'I'll go,' Lilia said, excusing herself.

A moment later, Lilia returned, holding her father's fedora with both hands, wrapping his overcoat over her forearm. Behind her was a slight, melanated man, barely taller than she. He carried a small parcel in a mustard-coloured envelope in his right hand and in the crook of his left arm, he held a bolt of deep red fabric. Sam(a) had never seen such a colour in Sam(a)'s reality, save perhaps an approximation of it on the cover of the Beach House album *Depression Cherry*, which was a fitting name for this colour, at once delicious and sad.

This was Sam(a)'s great grandfather, Ayoub. Sam(a) stood reflexively in respect for her ancestor, as Sam and Wassim had stood to say the mourners' קדיש - Kaddish prayer for him once each year, since Sam was a young child. Ayoub, taken aback by her abundance of deference, nodded and motioned with his package for her to sit down.

'My son, this is Sama. I know her well. She has come from so far away— From Mansoura! She's staying with us for the time being,' Hawa said, preempting an argument.

'I see,' Ayoub said. 'Sama, my girl, how is it you know my mother?' His voice was deep and commanding. There was a touch of honey to it. Sam(a) knew Ayoub to be an itinerant **חזן** - hazon - cantor at several synagogues in and around Alexandria . He was an accountant by trade, but he had retired b y his late 40s. Sam(a) understood, finally, why his musical services were so heavily in demand. He had a pleasant yet authoritative voice, like James Earl Jones would have after he was born, decades later.

Sam(a) looked at Hawa, still holding her hand. Sam(a) gently squeezed Hawa's hand as if to communicate gratitude for Hawa's lies.

'How I know her is a secret between women, son,' Hawa said. 'You have only to know that she is the daughter of someone close to this family from long ago. You have only to know that she is like a daughter to you and that she has nowhere else to go. She needs to stay with us. For some time.'

Ayoub stared at his mother, stern and calculating. Sam(a) felt Ayoub's patience was about to boil over. Hawa was expressionless. She spoke without hesitation. The lies had come too easy to her, Sam(a) remarked.

'You should not let there be pressure on a stranger — You have known the spirit of the stranger, for you had been strangers in the land of Egypt,' Wassim said to his father, in an Arabic-accented biblical Hebrew. With a passage from Exodus, Wassim had plunged everyone into thought. With these words, he had bound their treatment of Sam(a) to their commitments to their faith.

'Lilia, come with me,' Ayoub said, placing his package and parcel of cloth on the dining room table. 'Excuse us a moment,' he told Sam(a), looking in her direction but just past her. Sam(a) recognised this as the way she had seen — in Egypt and Tamazgha, in what had been Sam's present-day — pious Arab men of all faiths half-look at women. Believers of other ethnicities had similar ways of rendering people of the opposite sex translucent. Ayoub's half-awareness of her made Sam(a) feel at once comfortable and like she was bound to miss an opportunity to ever see this ancestor face-to-face.

In the moment of silence that set in the dining room while Ayoub and Lilia spoke in the kitchen, Sam(a) inspected the fabric across the table. It seemed like a safe space to rest her eyes without overstepping the bounds of some sort of etiquette she had not fully understood, even from the countless stories Wassim had told Sam(a) of Egypt. Then Sam(a)'s gaze turned to the package. It seemed like a curious little parcel, no larger than a booklet, bound with some twine string. Just as her eyes set upon it, Ayoub returned to the dining room and swiftly removed it from the table. The curiosity of his disapproval almost set Sam(a) to laughing, if only out of sheer awkwardness, but she restrained herself. Ayoub tucked the parcel, now electric with Sam(a)'s curiosity, under his right arm, and lifted a hand to bid the room goodbye. He left the bolt of fabric on the table.

Lilia who had been standing behind her father, approached the table to address Sam(a).

'Baba says we are to take you to Monsieur Edouard, the dressmaker,' Lilia said, laying a hand on the fabric. 'This is the fabric father received for his singing at the synagogue. We hope you like it.'

'It's beautiful. I can't accept this extravagance,' Sam(a) said, still marvelling at a colour that had disappeared in Sam(a)'s modern day. 'I am already indebted to you for letting me stay here awhile .'

'You are our guest — We're honoured that you are with us,' Lilia said. 'We can carry on this way for days, politely refusing each other, or we can run and see if Monsieur Edouard can finish a frock in time for Shabbat. There's no delicate way to ask this — Are you Jewish, Sama?'

'Like our ancestors and their children, thank Heaven,' Hawa proclaimed, before she took a hearty bite of the elusive cake that Lilia had intended for her guests. No one had seen her take a slice.

13. Have Fun Tonight

A magnetic force pulled Tony and I onto the beach just beyond the Russian boardwalk restaurant. It would have dragged us directly into the dark expanse of the Atlantic Ocean, if Tony had not suddenly seized me by the arm.

'What's wrong?' I asked, startled.

'Tonight is crazy enough, right?' Tony said.

I was uncertain that this had been a question. 'Crazy enough for what,' I asked.

We stood silently, for a moment, looking at each other, and then we simultaneously collapsed into o ne another's arms. My lips pressed deeply against Tony's cheeks as if to leave — with or without pain — a mark so firm that Tony would remember it. Tony matched my ferocity. We became as two mimes, mirroring the height of each other's passions. Eventually, we imploded to our knees. And finally, we were rolling in the sand with abandon.

A small beach patrol buggy approached the dark mass we had become and and an anxious-sounding civil servant with a loudspeaker notified us from a safe distance that the beach closes at dusk. We straightened ourselves up and returned, first to the boardwalk, then through an alleyway back to Brighton Beach Avenue.

'Is this a common occurrence, for you?' Tony asked.

'Is what a common occurrence?' I returned. 'Rolling around with people on Brighton Beach?'

'That and the madness of this evening, more generally,' Tony said.

I looked ahead, speechless. There was no fitting answer. Brighton Beach was what it was, every time. That night was a night apart, for altogether different reasons.

'Can't stop now. We have to up the ante!' Tony said.

Tony surveyed the shops on Brighton Beach Avenue. On a street corner, just past a pharmacy, he spied a psychic.

'Let's go get our fortunes told. What do you say?' Tony said. 'My treat. I've never been, and this night is a bit of everything.'

'I don't need my fortune told, but I'll watch you,' I said.

'Too far-out for you?' Tony asked.

'It's against my religion to know the future,' I said.

'You're religious!' Tony proclaimed, amused.

I looked at Tony with an exasperated silence.

'That's alright — You can listen to what will happen to me,' Tony said.

Tony opened the door to the psychic shop and a loud bell announced our entry. I felt trapped. Inside, we found a dark, spare room with just a round table draped in crushed emerald velvet, topped with a crystal ball on a silver-plated stand in the shape of a coiled cobra. In the corner of the room was a statue of a cat in the Ancient Egyptian style. I averted my eyes from it. Wassim would have said that this place was against Heaven.

'Минутку' - Minutku - Just a minute, a woman shouted over a blaring television set from a backroom behind the curtain.

Through a pair of shimmering black sequins curtains, she appeared, a caricature of a Southern Brooklyn woman. She wore a black turban over short, over-processed hair. Her microbladed eyebrows were fading into a light blue, like two prison tattoos announcing themselves prominently across the forehead. She wore a large peacock-feather-patterned shawl that she swung over her large, pendulous breasts before she took a seat.

'Hello, boys,' she said. 'I am Vanya, the seer. You are here for the $5 evening special, yes?'

'You would know,' Tony said, rifling through his messenger bag.

'Funny guy,' she said, pursing her lips, as she pulled a sack of esoteric accoutrements from a small bookcase under the table. '$5 for the cards, $20 for the ball, $100 for medium work.'

'Medium work, as in?' Tony asked. I felt my jaw clench.

'Communicating with your dearly departed' , Vanya said.

'Of course,' Tony said.

'He'll take the cards,' I interjected. Tony placed the cash on the table. Vanya took the cash and put it into the bookcase below the table.

Silently, in my mind, I repeatedly recited the שמע - Shema prayer — an attestation of monotheism to counter this place of idols and necromancy. I regretted having developed a relationship to anyone or thing in Brighton Beach beyond its Uyghur dumplings. I was paying the price for this dalliance with Tony — for involving myself too deeply in humanity. Vanya shuffled her cards and retrieved three, which she laid on the table, face up. I did not dare look at them too closely.

'That's not right,' she said, reshuffling the cards. She furrowed her brow.

'Oh?' Tony asked, still amused. 'Well that doesn't sound promising.'

'Not to worry,' she said. 'Answer me this — There is something strange between you two. You are boys who like boys, yes?'

We stared at her blankly.

'You are boys who like boys. You have something strange between the two of you. Some things you do not know, perhaps,' she said.

'We just met,' I said.

'Yes, yes,' Vanya said, satisfied. She looked directly at me. 'May I hold your hand?'

A full second of total inertia — save the static sound of panic ringing in my ears — passed.

'I am very sorry, Ms. Vanya— I can't,' I said.

'You can hold my hand,' Tony interjected, extending his hand toward her as if to accept an invitation to dance.

'Very well,' Vanya said, eyes fixed on me as she took Tony's hand and flipped it to read his palm.

'Soft hand,' she said, with a snide smile. Vanya closed her eyes and turned her head up to face the ceiling, from whence her special knowledge came.

'This what I am going to tell you now, boys — This is important and no more charge, you understand?' she said.

Tony and I looked at her, blankly.

'Unless you want to pay more, that is also O.K.,' she said, looking back down at us, frustrated. Tony smiled and shook his head no. She returned her head to the ceiling and closed her eyes once again.

'Three words, boys, and what lies between them,' she said. 'Have fun tonight.'

And with that she arose, gave us a little bow with prayer hands, and retreated behind the black sequinned curtain, back to her television set. She returned the volume to what it had been before we arrived.

Tony and I looked at each other. Tony was on the verge of laughter. I felt a queasiness in my stomach. My brow had furrowed. We collected ourselves and stood to go.

'Have fun tonight!' Vanya shouted once more.

'Thank you!' Tony shouted back on our way out. A great ocean wind pulled the shop door wide open and then slammed it shut behind us.

A chill had set into Brighton Beach Avenue and its byways.

'Remarkable, that,' Tony said. 'You repeat anything enough times and it sounds spooky. "Have fun tonight"'.

I was deep in thought.

'Do you live nearby?' I asked, ignoring Tony's quip.

'No, I live out in Astoria,' he said.

'I see— I'm on the Lower East Side,' I said, looking down to the ground.

'Are you alright?' Tony asked.

'Yes, I was just thinking maybe we should head back to one of our places,' I said.

'You don't seem very excited about it,' Tony said. 'And what's the rush — You still have to show me Brighton. Was it the psychic? Did she freak you out?'

'It's such a long story,' I said. 'We don't have the time'.

A man walking into the pharmacy next door to Vanya's psychic shop took a final, heartfelt drag of his cigarette and flicked it out into the street before pulling open the heavy swinging door. I felt a pressure in my head and then synapses falling into place. I looked in both directions for our next destination. I yawned deeply — a yawning of the soul.

'There it is again — your deep sighing, like you're out of breath,' Tony said. 'You wanna tell me what's up before we go back to anyone's place?'

'I don't want to tell you too much and ruin this evening for us both,' I said.

'How might the truth ruin our evening?' Tony asked.

'Maybe you'd hear it and float away down one of these side streets,' I said.

'Maybe,' Tony said. 'Or maybe it wouldn't make a difference. Why don't you try me?'

'Fine then,' I said, looking down at my shoes. The wind assaulted our ears. 'Let's go have a slice of cake and some coffee, shall we? I'll tell you all there is to know.'

'Alright,' Tony said, 'But maybe you could start now, since you're freaking me out, and we're in a strange neighbourhood of Brooklyn, after dark'.

'Fair enough,' I said. 'First, I should say: Tonight is my last night in Brighton'.

'Are you dying?' Tony asked. 'What does that mean?'

'It means have fun tonight.'

14. A Light
Du Feu

At our first session, when Doctor Fahmy asked why I wanted to quit smoking, I thought she was kidding. I was one of the last smokers left alive. People reviled me on the sidewalks of New York, particularly at a time of heightened attention to healthful living marked by a sudden proliferation of organic food shops and yoga studios in formerly working-class neighbourhoods.

To my mind, Doctor Fahmy's need to know why I wanted to quit called into question whether hypnosis was a kind of therapy. Otherwise, the why would not have mattered, only my desired outcome. I suppose I feared from the start that hypnotherapy was therapy — It announces itself as such. And like analysis, hypnotherapy is designed to fix problems rooted deeply in the psyche — for money.

I had chosen Doctor Fahmy's hypnotherapy practice in Bay Ridge because a social worker friend had explained to me once that it is helpful to see mental health professionals of your own ethnic background. I expected that Doctor Fahmy would intuit certain things about me — certain normal, little things that another practitioner might find to be idiosyncratic and strange, like my inescapable fear of the Evil Eye and the way my life had been lived in service of my grandparents. I chose her so I could explain and speak less. And yet, she for some reason chose to ask why I was there. I felt the answer should have been self-evident, regardless of my ethnicity or religion. I was there to do something every smoker should want to do.

When I looked at her blankly, Doctor Fahmy reshaped the question. She broke it down into two: Why had I started smoking? And where would it lead? These questions pleased me. Where do you come from? and Where are you going? are two questions we asked every year at our Passover table — customarily, as a sort of post-prayer game. I assume Doctor Fahmy was not Jewish, but she had successfully translated her approach into terms I could understand. The Saadoun family's answers to the Passover set of questions were never serious. We were a family of exiles. The answer to the first question was that European colonial projects had ripped us from our homeland in Egypt, and we had been looking for home ever since, including in the most self-destructive ways. Still, no one thought to answer these questions in a realistic or a politically meaningful way. We spoke of bourgeois and pleasant things: The dinner table of that moment was where we came from, and we always wished to someday see the clash of artfully manicured nature and electrified commerce that makes Tokyo or the otherworldly astral soup of the Northern Lights in Iceland.

I felt that Dr. Fahmy had — probably unwittingly — made her interrogation Egyptian and Jewish enough for me to hear it. So I decided to entertain her rephrased questions.

Where does the smoking come from? From the whole world's collective imagination of a certain kind of woman. I started smoking thanks to:

1. Brigitte Lin Qing-hsia, *Chungking Express*, 1994: In this iconic Wong Kar-wai film, Lin portrays a poetic mobster who wears a blonde wig, a trench coat, and sunglasses. Her character is cool and dangerous and ultimately reveals herself as a decolonialism symbol. In one scene, in between dodging adversaries, the mobster luxuriously smokes an old-fashioned, pink cigarette and beholds the languid smoke rising from her mouth. Her cigarettes signify that no matter the outcome of her running, she is unconcerned with life, in the long-term.

2. Jessica Lange, *American Horror Story*, Coven, 2013: Lange is the queen of the witches. She uses her cigarette to point for emphasis, in the way American TV witches point to do magic. Her cigarette is a wand. She also uses her cigarette to express displeasure with people. Her cigarette is an expression of nonchalance and her disinterest in her own life and the lives of others. She'll smoke right in your face. A bad bitch and a force to be reckoned with.

3. Kerri Russell, *The Americans* on FX Season 6, 2018: Russell portrays an undercover Soviet intelligence agent in Washington, D.C. under the Reagan administration. With the authorities closing in on her, she becomes an unrelenting chainsmoker. She also begins to wear a cyanide pill in a locket around her neck. She is unafraid of the end. In fact, it appears that she is actively trying to lessen any time she may spend in a maximum security prison or on Death Row.

'Movies,' I told Doctor Fahmy, instead of the above list of femmes fatales. The list of para-suicidal Hollywood lady mobsters is endless.

With my smoking, I had retreated into cinema. I had done so for more than two hours — I had been a smoker for a decade. Part of me knew I was not as tough as the persona I had styled after these strong female leads. I was living a fantasy, posing as people who pose as people for a living, in the same pitiful way that hipsters in hipster enclaves around the world pose as other posers in Williamsburg, Brooklyn. I posed, to myself in my mind's eye, as a powerful woman, using frivolous paper props that became a prison.

When I held my cigarette between my index and middle fingers, I was graceful and feminine. When I held my cigarette between my thumb and index finger, I was a fun masculine feminine person. I was a tomboy — cinema and straight male society's preferred sort of woman or feminine gay man. I was the kind of femme person who can hang with the boys. If I pointed my cigarette directly at a person while I made the key points of an argument, the cigarette became as a magic wand or a laser pointer or a switchblade. If I was breaking up with someone — typically, before they would could break up with me — the burning paper and tobacco became whatever we had, up in ashes. If I needed an excuse to speak to someone interesting, I asked for a light. In a family where we never discussed sexuality, I learned from films that cigarettes are bookends to intimacy — an opening line, a means of drawing attention to one's little ballet of machinations, and a punctuation mark at the end of fornication. A decompression. A cooling down exercise, powered by fire and nicotine.

Running alongside the women of our movies, there was an altogether different and simultaneous reason for my smoking that gave it a sort of sanctity. There was Wassim. His cigarettes and coffee were the mornings from long ago, before I could remember sorrow. Even when I was not actively thinking of Wassim, something about the smell of my cigarette smoke mingling with the smell of freshly brewed coffee communicated love to me, in my studio on Manhattan's Lower East Side, years after Wassim had died, and I had finally left our apartment in Brooklyn.

So the cigarettes were at once the futurism of my homosexuality and femininity, so unlike our family in their refusal of our faith and machismo, and they were also of the distant past, reviving a dead person who had raised me.

Eventually, somewhere between the two, I forgot how to breathe on my own. Smoking had become like meditation — a reminder, however toxic, to inhale and exhale. I knew to take a pause from the workday only because I had to smoke once every other hour, during my waking hours. And the act of smoking seemed to normalise my naturally erratic, anxious breathing, even if those breaths became progressively shallow as my lungs grew weaker.

I explained some approximation of these things to Doctor Fahmy. She made brief notes on her pad, as we sat in her little pantry-office. The notes were so brief in fact that I wondered if very little of what I said had been significant to her. Or perhaps her notes were just a formality, and my act of recollection was itself a step or a ritual in her hypnosis.

Doctor Fahmy then reiterated her second question: 'And where is the smoking going? Where is the smoker you — the you of right now — headed?'

'Death,' I said. I felt a jolt in my chest. 'The understanding has always been that I was committing a sort of slow, public act of suicide.'

'And you no longer want to do that anymore — to kill yourself publicly?' she asked.

'I want to breathe,' I said. 'For now. For now, I want to breathe big, old breaths — deep, full breaths. I am ready to feel life with the whole of my chest again.'

I was already in a sedate mood. Doctor Fahmy took me down with her even further. First with the numbers. She counted back from ten. Halfway through, there was a small pause, like an elongated landing at the middle of a staircase.

I remember only moments of what transpired during the formal part of the hypnosis. Doctor Fahmy said at one point that whenever I felt the urge to smoke, my lungs would fill with air, and when I exhaled, I would forget entirely the desire to smoke. I had planned to light up just outside of her apartment building in Bay Ridge, right after our session. But then I must have yawned my way down the block and simply forgotten to smoke again.

The rest of the hypnosis was a sensation akin to when I had my wisdom teeth pulled on heavy-duty drugs — I was far out. I couldn't even hear Doctor Fahmy's voice. All I recall of those moments is auras of splendid colours that I have never experienced in real life, even in kaleidoscopes.

I wonder if the kaleidoscope was what Wassim saw when they gave him the morphine in his final hours?

15. Have Fun Tonight

'Hypnotherapy for smoking cessation,' Tony said, between bites of вареники - vareniki cherry dumplings, slathered in so much sour cream that their sweet and tart innards turned a lovely Soviet pink.

We sat at a table at the very front of Skovorodka, a Russian restaurant on the main drag of Brighton Beach Avenue. Before me was Tony, behind him was a window to the street. And in front of that window, on the sidewalk, was the backside of a large statue of a ferocious Russian bear showing its fangs. The bear wore a lovely plaque around his neck inviting customers to enter. I had taken a cup of coffee and a large rectangular slice of Napoleon cake. I had touched neither. I had busied my mouth with an explanation of my sighs.

'Interesting. And how did that work for you?' Tony said, as skeptical as he had been at the fortuneteller. I found him to be as frustratingly smug in that moment as Vanya the Soothsayer probably had.

'Surprisingly well!' I said. 'Quitting was still hard. I gained weight, and I'm still irritable sometimes. Maybe I'd have been fat and angry even if hadn't quit smoking, to be real with myself. But I stopped smoking almost a year ago. Haven't touched a cigarette since.'

'Well done you,' Tony said. 'That explains the yawning,

but it doesn't explain tonight. You sound like tonight is your last night to live.'

I took a bite of my Napoleon. Tony had taken a pause from his cherry dumplings to stare at me. To my mind, he was the sort of sharp-elbowed British person who enjoyed holding my feet to the fire. I was the sort of petulant, childish American who would not let him win. I took a sip of my coffee, the hue and flavour of dishwater.

'You ask me all sorts of questions, and you've yet to say a single thing about yourself,' I said.

'You've yet to ask,' Tony said, returning to his dumplings.

'Fair enough. I wanna know why you're still around.'

Tony laughed. 'I suppose I'd have to be nuts to want to be around you?' Tony asked with a wry smile.

I didn't know how to respond. I looked at my cake.

'Hey, sir — Look at me,' Tony said. 'Where do you go when you look down like that? Like a mournful Virgin Mary?'

I smiled. 'If I were sort of extravagantly good-looking, maybe you could overlook the fact that I'm not exactly a barrel of laughs,' I said.

'Who's to say you're not a barrel of laughs to me?' Tony replied.

'Wrong answer. You should have immediately responded that I am indeed extravagantly good-looking,' I said, half-serious.

'So you're fishing for compliments?' Tony returned.

A moment passed.

'You're beautiful,' I said.

Tony looked down at his cherry dumplings, exaggeratedly sullen. He took a sorrowful bite and let the bit of dumpling drop from his mouth to the table.

'Funny guy,' I said. 'Vanya the Soothsayer called it.'

'You do realise that Vanya the Soothsayer was bound to end up saying vaguely intuitive shit like, "You guys look gay together— You guys don't know everything there is to know about each other— Have fun tonight". That's how psychics work. Everyone knows that, Sam — Everyone who believes in science and reality. The psychics read a few cues from how you look and cook up something both vague and universally true enough to be applicable to situations they know nothing about.'

I felt calm, when he said this.

'Can you hold my hand?' I asked.

Tony put his hand palm up beside my Napoleon. He had beautiful hands. Delicate, well-manicured fingers.

'Under the table,' I specified. Tony looked upset. 'This neighbourhood voted overwhelmingly for Trump,' I explained.

He put his hand under the table. We both reached awkwardly to link the tips of our fingers.

A few years prior, I had dated a man — half French, half Egyptian, worked in finance or some other soulless thing. He also seemed not to care than I was a constitutionally anxious person. He loved to put his hand on my waist as we walked, to feel the excess of me jiggle. One day, we met up for drinks after work at the Boiler Room, not far from where I lived, and I spied him spying someone more conventionally pleasant. So I told him I'm descended from a long line of powerfully Resentful Egyptian women. The dude looked confused. I went outside and smoked. I watched my insides evaporate into the crystalline night sky. When we said goodbye that night, it was goodbye forever. There were only a few calls and texts I left unanswered before I had snuffed him out— before he could do the same.

'My arm is sore,' I told Tony, retracting my hand. 'Thank you for indulging me.' Nothing under Heaven stays. He remained awkwardly bent, one arm reaching out for me under the table for a moment. I wanted to go back for him. But a moment passed, and he retracted his arm.

'Tomorrow, this won't matter,' I began. 'It's cosmically perfect that tonight I should meet someone so charming and soulful, as a parting kick in the teeth.'

Tony sat in silence, waiting for more.

'The other day, I was here in Brighton, on the beach at dusk, and I thought: "I have no family left in this place. My career is whatever. I don't have anything keeping me here. I should go back to Egypt",' I said.

'What would you do there?' Tony asked. 'Do you have anything there? Family? A job?'

'Nothing. I have nothing. Nothing but all my ancestors' decaying bones under my feet from time immemorial,' I said. 'I've looked into jobs. I guess I'd teach English or something. Doesn't matter how much it pays; I don't need a whole lot to get by anymore.'

'So you're leaving?' Tony said. 'You fly out tomorrow or?'

'No, no,' I said.

'Then meet me back here for dinner — back at Kashkar,' Tony said. I felt this comment spawn something like delight in my chest. And then I remembered he would eventually still be a man.

'No, I'll be gone, in another sense,' I said. 'This is where you leave, probably. I reached out to Doctor Fahmy to see if she could adjust her smoking cessation hypnotherapy to stop me from being— from wanting sex.'

'Oh,' Tony said, sitting upright. 'Like gay conversion therapy?'

'No, no — There's a big difference between what I'm doing and that. And why.'

'There is?' Tony said, visibly exasperated.

'I need to go back,' I said. 'I don't want to let my sexuality get in the way. I've spent enough time pursuing things with men, and I've never had a single one show me the kind of family I want. I know that if I go home, I'll find it there. Sex isn't everything. In fact, the older I get, the more it seems like an obstacle to what I need.'

'You wanted to go back to one of our flats, just now?' Tony asked, perplexed.

'Maybe you've had the experience of being someone's first, but have you ever been a guy's last?'

'Ha!' Tony ejected, in a single burst of breath. 'A smarter man would leave you here and chalk this up to that one crazy fucking night with a crazy fucker in Brighton.'

'Aren't therapists not supposed to call people crazy?' I asked.

Tony smiled. Everyone's patience has a limit. Even the therapists, great Western bastions of calm and sobriety, have a breaking point.

'Leave me here,' I said. 'It would make things easier.'

I looked at my cake. My fork danced along the cream and pâte feuilletée, leaving little impressions. I wanted to take my hand, crush it. Hard. I wanted to ball it up into little

Napoleon falafels, in the way that non-Arabs make chocolate-chip-cookie-flavoured hummus, in the way babies make ice cream soup. But I restrained myself out of pity for Tony. He had seen and heard enough for one evening. Poor man.

'Doctor Fahmy agreed to do this asexualising hypnotherapy?' Tony said.

'I told her I was a sex addict,' I said. 'I told her it was an emergency. That I was a nymphomaniac — sometimes five men a day. Strangers in alleyways. And that I needed to end it, altogether. Something final. A full stop.'

'I see,' Tony said, deep in thought. He looked at his half-eaten dumplings and then straight into my eyes. I felt seized and shaken by his intensity. 'Well, I guess Vanya the Soothsayer got lucky this time. We had better have a whole lot of fun, right? And fast.'

I inhaled a chestful of air. But I hadn't noticed any smokers passing Skovorodka on Brighton Beach Avenue.

16. A Trap فخ

Sam(a) hummed a vaguely familiar tune. It lingered just out of reach — only a few notes, repeating in her mind and mouth. She waited for Lilia and Ghozala to ready themselves to pay a visit to Monsieur Edouard, the dressmaker. Whatever the song stuck in her mind had been, it nourished feelings of melancholy in her chest.

Hawa left through the front door with the three young women, back onto Flower Street. As they made their way up the block, in the opposite direction of the Mediterranean, Hawa made a sharp left, down the alleyway beside their home, back into the garden from which she had emerged with Sam(a) the night before. At the entryway to the alley was a marble arch, two short Corinthian columns upholding a marble banner with a relief of three oversized jasmine buds, intertwined with ribbon. It was a half-hearted attempt at something regal to mask an otherwise ominous-looking passageway between the Saadoun family home and their neighbours.

'Where is she going?' Sam(a) asked. In a short space of time, a piece of Sam(a)'s soul seemed to have attached itself to Hawa, the first person she had met in Alexandria, the person who had pulled her into that place and time.

'She lives with our grandfather in a small apartment we built for them behind the home,' Lilia explained. 'It's a small

space. It's probably why she wanders the neighbourhood
like a madwoman. Claustrophobia.'

Sam(a) recalled that Wassim would later tell Sam that
his family had constructed a small apartment for Hawa
and her husband behind their home. To look at the
physical layout of their family's property, it appeared
to Sam(a) that they had hidden their forebears in the
back yard. Wassim would never have admitted to such
a thing, but Sam(a) had sensed a certain condescension
or resentment from the Saadoun children toward their
grandparents. Hawa — and her husband Adam, judging
by the photo of him in Sam(a)'s childhood apartment
in Brooklyn — dressed and behaved like their ancestors
always had, before a series of European conquests. It was
as though Hawa and Adam were certain that concepts of
Europe as progress and the future were a passing fashion.
What if they were right? Sam(a) thought. It seemed that the
Saadouns had gone so far West that Sam(a) had snapped
right back to Egypt.

The young women passed a flower shop, capitalising on
the street's name to sell resplendent bouquets wrapped
in light pink paper. Sam(a) began to hum again. This
time, she recognised the tune. She had been humming
Will You Still Love Me Tomorrow. Ghozala, who had been
walking silently a few paces ahead of Lilia and Sam(a),
carrying the deep red fabric in both arms , shot Sam(a)
a look as Sam(a) hummed. Sam(a) noticed Ghozala's left
eye twitch. The minuscule muscles around her left eye
seized up briefly and then released. Sam(a) read her face.
Ghozala smiled politely and looked away.

From Flower Street, the Saadoun women crossed Tigran Basha, a larger avenue. There, Sam(a) found apartment buildings and on the ground floor of several of them, a series of food vendors. A sandwich counter, a small grocery, an ice cream shop. The shops bore signs in French and frequently — although not always — in smaller Arabic script. Finally, the women turned right on Sidi Gaber, a large avenue with broad sidewalks. A single motorcar passed, and then a moment later, there was a double-decker tram pulling into a nearby station. The people alighting were all men, wearing an array of different outfits: Some wore جلابية - galabeya cloaks, others wore suits, and the younger and more foppish men wore short trousers to their nipples and high socks to their knees. A few minutes into their trek on Sidi Gaber, they arrived at a shop painted a regal forest green, announcing itself in golden lettering as *Monsieur Edouard et Cie, Couturier* مسيو إدوارد - ملابس - . Lilia rang a doorbell that made a loud, shrill buzz. No one answered, so she rang a second time. Through the glass panel in the door, there were two scarlet velour curtains. A short, stout man with a handlebar moustache peaked through, holding the curtains under his chin like a headscarf.

'How can I help you, ladies?' the man said.

'Oh, hello, Mister Hani,' Lilia said, a bit startled. 'Can Mister Ilyas see us this afternoon, please? We need to have a dress made for our cousin from Mansoura.'

'I'm afraid not, Ms. Lilia,' Hani said. 'Mister Ilyas is quite preoccupied and will not be available for the rest of the day. Come back tomorrow.' And with that, he was gone.

The ladies strolled back toward Flower Street, with less purpose now.

'He seemed a bit curt, didn't he?' Ghozala said.

'A bit,' said Lilia. 'But it's not his fault. We should have expected there would be no availability ahead of the weekend.'

'There's no Monsieur Edouard at Monsieur Edouard and Company?' Sam(a) asked.

'There is indeed a Monsieur Edouard,' Lilia said. 'Monsieur Edouard is a very busy and an important man. He's a Swiss! He owns several ateliers in Alexandria and Cairo. He is not the sort of man who sits in a shop in Sidi Gaber sewing dresses. He employs people to do that for him.'

'I see, and this is a popular clothing store, for you?' Sam(a) asked.

'My, you ask a lot of questions!' Lilia said. 'I assure you that you will find their clothes to be up to your standards.'

Sam(a) feared that she was making an enemy of Lilia. It was easy, with the Saadouns, to offend. The Saadouns felt with the whole of their chests. Their highs and lows formed canyons. Their Resentments were firm as sediment. The Saadoun family experienced an unexamined sympathy for elephants in their family, likely both because elephants and the Saadouns were very family oriented and because they never forgot it when they feel they'd been wronged.

'I am absolutely certain they are wonderful dresses! I don't know very much about such things,' Sam(a) said.

'What girl doesn't know Monsieur Edouard? Are you simple?' Lilia asked.

'Lilia!' Ghozala said. 'There are indeed people who don't know about Monsieur Edouard. Sama meant you no offence.'

Lilia looked into Ghozala's eyes for a tense moment. Ghozala held her gaze. A challenge.

'Are you hungry?' Lilia asked Sam(a). 'You must try Mister Ramzi's shawarma on Tigran Basha Street.'

Sam(a) had eaten a great deal that morning — fava beans and chocolate cake for breakfast. They were already making themselves known as unlikely bedfellows in her stomach. And now Lilia would feed her greasy meat. Sam(a) wondered what toilets looked like in 1930s Alexandria. Were they holes in the ground or European-style potties? There are questions you never ask your grandparents. For instance, in that moment, Sam(a) was not wearing a bra. Lilia had simply not offered her one. Sam(a) was uncertain that bras existed at that time. She was uncertain why women wore bras in the modern-day. Would her breasts begin to hurt or perspire without one? And if Sam(a) raised these issues to Lilia and Ghozala, would they laugh or find her to be even more uncouth?

Sam(a) agreed to the shawarma sandwich. Sam(a) had never met Lilia, who had died before he was born. But he recalled that his grandmother had once visited Lilia's apartment in Queens. Lilia had prepared بامية - bamia - stewed okra with rice for lunch, and Sam(a)'s grandmother had just eaten before coming to call. 'I'll have to feed it to the cat,' Lilia said, removing the casserole from her dining room table, looking away from Sam(a)'s grandmother. This gave Sam(a)'s grandmother pause, because Lilia had no cat. Sam(a)'s grandmother was never again invited over for lunch.

There was no sign above Mister Ramzi's shop. It was a hole in the wall — a counter, before three large stacks of meat, rotating on spits. In the back room, behind a drawn curtain with grease stains, a radio blared. The ladies stood at the counter for a few moments.

'Mister Ramzi, hello?' Lilia called out over the din.

A shrill voice, full of static called back to her from the radio:

زورونى كل سنه مرة
حرام تنسونى بالمرة -

Visit me once a year
It would be shameful if you suddenly forget me

'Hello!' Lilia called again. 'Mister Ramzi, Hello! We would like a sandwich!'

No one answered. Sam(a) was relieved.

'What's happening today?' Lilia said in a huff. 'No one in Sidi Gaber has time for us, I suppose.'

On their way home, the girls passed the florist of Flower Street. A shop worker, short and slight with fair skin and a head of tight, dark curls, handed Sam(a) a single rosebud. No words. Just a smile. Sam(a) searched his face, then looked at the flower.

'Thank you!' Sam(a) exclaimed.

Lilia, who had been walking with Ghozala just ahead of Sam(a), turned back.

'Oh yes, how kind of you,' Lilia told the florist. She grabbed Sam(a)'s arm and hurried her along toward the Saadoun's house on Flower Street.

'It seems some people in Sidi Gaber have time for us,' Ghozala said.

Back home, sitting around the kitchen table, the deep red bolt of fabric lying on the table, Lilia served the three girls coffee. Wassim had left to his job with a foreign shipping company.

'Sama, my dear,' Lilia said. 'You are a pretty girl, thank Heaven. Lovely, in your way.'

'That's kind,' Sam(a) said.

'But we don't speak to strange men on the street,' Lilia continued.

Ghozala fixed her eyes on Sam(a).

'What should I have done? He offered me a flower,' Sam(a) asked.

'Don't be upset, dear Sama,' Lilia said. 'I say this for your own good. If our neighbours saw you speaking to strange men, imagine what they'd start saying about the women of this house. Especially since we're all unmarried.'

'Maybe I'm just ignorant of social graces. What should I have said?' Sam(a) asked.

'You should have nodded, smiled, and passed,' Lilia said. 'It's that simple. When a man gives you a flower, he is not doing it out of kindness, Sama. He is doing it because he has ideas.'

'I see,' Sam(a) said.

A moment later, Sam(a) helped Lilia clear the table when they had finished their coffee and began to wash dishes for the first time at an unfamiliar sink. She thought of the man's smile. He was not unhandsome. Sam(a) wondered how long she would live in that reality. She wondered about the florist. *Was it more than a flower? Had he wanted to have sex?*

It occurred to Sam(a) that she would be an idiot not to experience sex as a woman. In high school, back in 21st century Brooklyn, she read the Greek myth of Tiresias, who had experienced sex as both a man and a woman and determined that it was better as a woman. Sam(a) was resolved in that moment to know what straight sex was for a woman. She wondered how much time she had left in 1930s Alexandria — how much time left she had in that body — before she returned to Sam in 21st century Brooklyn. She felt a great sense of urgency to her sexual mission: She had to get laid, and fast. What's worse, she wondered how it could ever happen — not the act itself, but when and where she would have sex in such a time and place — and without ruining the Saadouns' reputation. It had always been so easy to go on Pound, the gay hook-up app, in 21st century Brooklyn. Sam(a) felt overwhelmed with both anxiety and desire. Bound and gagged. She wondered if any of her matriarchs had ever wanted to have sex. And what if they felt an urgent and visceral need to have sex, like Sam(a) in that moment. What happened to them? Did they hide it away until it no longer existed, or did they meet some sort of horrible end?

Sam(a) looked through a window above the kitchen sink that showed the back yard from whence Hawa had pulled Sam(a) into her reality. She beheld the small apartment at the centre of the garden where her great-great-grandparents lived, tucked away like their past. And wandering around the small dwelling, in a sort of sorrowful pacing, a bit rhythmic like a dance, was Hawa, the ghost of the garden of the House on Flower Street.

17. Russian Dolls матрешки

'We are closing — 20 minutes,' said a shop worker whose name tag read Ludmila. I'd describe Ludmila's physicality to a forensic sketch artist as 'unenthusiastic.' She wore a dress shirt, some slacks, and a felt кокóшник - kokoshnik cap that recast her expressionless head as the flamboyant, sainted dome of a Russian Orthodox cathedral.

Anadyr Art and Souvenir was a large emporium on Brighton Beach Avenue with mannequins in the shop windows dressed as Cossacks and Russian princesses wearing kokoshniks like Ludmila's. Ludmila took Tony's messenger bag at the entrance and put it in a small cubby. In exchange, she gave him a little laminated number with which he could retrieve his belongings. Ludmila and her bosses would not abide the petty theft of their Russian curios.

'That's five of our 20 minutes, checking your bag,' I told Tony, under my breath.

'We'd better make those 15 minutes count,' Tony said, beholding a wall of матрешки - matryoshki - nesting dolls of various sizes in vivid colours — mostly shiny, lacquered reds and oranges like painted bell peppers, but also a sprinkling of blue winter ladies, studded with glittered snowflakes. Featured prominently at the right of the matryoshka display were several political matryoshka dolls — robust Putins. An open one revealed a Yeltsin and a Gorbachev. And beside them was a Trump doll, whose contents were uncertain.

'It assaults the eyes, doesn't it?' I said, my dazzled gaze marvelling at the dizzying lacquered rainbow before us.

'I wonder what the market for this crap is?' Tony asked.

'Not into souvenirs?' I asked.

'No — never a fan of a tchotchke,' he replied. 'I find that clutter clutters my mind. Especially in these tight New York flats.'

'Your apartment must be very neat,' I said.

'Maybe you'll find out,' he said.

This was a kind of coy I found unattractive.

'I like these Russian dolls — I don't know why,' I said.

'There's a sort of poetry to them, isn't there?' Tony said.

'Several simultaneous people, living all at once,' I said.

'Are they coexisting, or do they consume each other?' he replied.

'Well that's a claustrophobic thought, Tony,' I said. 'Try to lighten up.'

I wonder if he received this as sarcasm. I had intended it as sarcasm, but it's difficult to read sarcasm, particularly in a different accent.

'If you leave it on a shelf somewhere and never let the little ladies out, do those little ladies exist at all?' Tony asked. 'Does a tree falling in the forest make a sound?'

'I'd have thought you'd love Russian nesting dolls. Aren't shrinks all about getting to the core of people?'

Tony did not respond. This had admittedly been a stupid observation.

We browsed propaganda posters from the Soviet Union. In one poster, a neat-looking blond man categorically refused to take a drink with his meal. 'нет!' - Nyet! - No! the poster shouted in an aggressive, red font. Beside the posters was a rack of novelty T-shirts. There was a novelty shirt of Soviet rock band Kino featuring the face of frontman Viktor Tsoi. Tsoi was attractive in a way befitting an iconoclastic Soviet rocker — sunken eyes and cheeks and an 80s mullet. Another T-shirt would announce the wearer — in big red characters — as 'КГБ' - KGB. Then there were a whole lot of T-shirts not readily discernible as adoring or ridiculing Vladimir Putin. 'Who's your Vladdy?' one T-shirt read, with a photo of a shirtless Putin on horseback.

On a display table next to the children's toys — baby dolls with mildly nightmarish faces and some stuffed dolls of Чебурáшка - Cheburashka, a Soviet cartoon character like a monkey with unnaturally large eyes and ears — was a display of the same photo of a shirtless Putin on horseback. There were mugs, calendars, keychains, coasters, ashtrays, all bearing the same photo of a half-nude Putin on horseback or another shirtless photo, likely from later that same day.

'I'm beginning to sense a theme,' Tony said, beholding Putin's stiff, hairless nipples on a car deodoriser.

I joined Tony in inspecting Putin's nipples very closely.

'How long do you think it'd take us to get back to one of our places if we took a taxi?' I asked.

'Really? This is what does it for you?' Tony asked. 'Vladdy Putin.'

'You're poking fun? You've been ogling his man boobs on that air freshener for a hot second,' I returned.

'Hot indeed,' Tony said. 'It'll be rush hour for at least another hour or two.'

Pressed for time, I retrieved my mobile phone from my back pocket.

'Do you know how expensive an Uber would be right now?' Tony said. 'We could take a town car, but it'll still cost us a fortune.'

I opened Pound, the gay hook-up app.

'What are you up to?' Tony said.

'If you're down, we could find someone around here who could host us,' I said. 'If you're into it. I could leave my Pound on while we keep walking around Brighton, see if anyone hits us up.'

'Depends on who it is, really,' Tony said. 'And what he's doing while we're doing it.'

'Just a third wheel — someone with a place nearby,' I said.

'In French it's — aptly, I should say — called, "quelqu'un qui tient la chandelle",' Tony said.

'Someone who what's the what?'

'"Someone who holds the candle" — A guest star.'

18. Origin Story

When he turned 4, Young Tony — still Brighton at the time — had a Little Mermaid-themed birthday party.

Young Brighton's parents were artists. When his mother, born to a couple of socialist philosophy professors in Mexico City, took British citizenship, both of his parents voted Labour. They cultivated and encouraged their son's feminine sensibility. They took long walks and discussed his feelings on all sorts of topics, including his gender identity. He was a very masculine feminine being, they decided, after years of discussions.

His parents made mistakes, as young people do. Take for instance Young Tony's Little Mermaid birthday. It was an extravagance of the most absurd kind. A paid actress was stranded in a chair at their local park, flapping her sequinned costume tail while insolent, little children prodded her for hours with their sticky, little frosting-coated hands. Before the children had been at it, the cake had been as a work of art — a pile of food-coloured blood sugar replicating the Little Mermaid statue of Copenhagen. One of the parents attending the party with her son suggested to Little Brighton's mother that the cake, which had very realistic nipples, was in poor taste at a children's birthday party. To this, Young Brighton's mother replied, as she removed her top, that the parent was free to remove her son from the party and that there is no fundamental difference between men's and women's nipples beyond oppressive social conventions. Young Brighton was embarrassed. But the fault was not in his mother's toplessness or their son's momentary embarrassment; it was in his parents' lust for feeding their child's costly appetites. Tony wanted for nothing, and when he hit puberty and his adult hormones began to introduce themselves, he was sharply shocked by the depression and anxiety that most people experience. He suddenly became very disillusioned and pensive.

A decade after the Little Mermaid birthday party, at an intensive poetry summer camp in Digne, in the South of France, Little Brighton — who had become Tony — read Baudelaire and wrote of the interplay between darkness and light. Obscure poems with hazy images. In that year's radius of blossoming poets was Augustín, a few years Tony's senior, from an aristocratic family living in Pozuelo de Alarcón, on the edge of Madrid. The two young men shared their first kiss on the outskirts of town. That same evening, they swapped roommates with the camp counsellors' approval.

After that summer, Augustín visited Tony in London. Tony's parents were very welcoming and understood entirely the nature of their relationship. Tony's mother in particular was happy to have another Spanish-speaker in the house and took Augustín on a whirlwind tour of the city. But the spark of the previous summer had fizzled out. When Augustín left, Tony felt relieved. He eventually stopped answering Augustín's correspondence, and at least for Tony, what they had faded into pleasant memories of a summer of awakening.

Sam and Tony grazed each other in June 2009. It was Pride, Tony's first in New York. He had just moved from

London for school. He was shirtless, frolicking among a sea of sweating bodies. Sam was trying to cross the parade route near New York University on Fifth Avenue to get to Jackson Diner, an all-you-can-eat Indian cuisine buffet. Sam rather aggressively knocked into Tony, compounding Tony's mounting feelings of resentment for New York City and the United States beyond it. Tony would eventually come to love the city. He would also begin to wear suits, even in the summertime, and avoid things like Pride, because he felt it to be what he frequently described to his friends as 'a mess.' He had become a psychologist — distinguished. Sam still stress-ate between journalism jobs — and still frequently at Jackson Diner, but the branch on Fifth Avenue near New York University had closed, so he went to the one in Queens.

Sam lost his virginity when he was 22, in the back of the small Toyota sedan belonging to a man nearly twice his age. The car was parked near a warehouse in the Sunset Park neighbourhood of Brooklyn, with a view of the Statue of Liberty and the Manhattan skyline in the distance. Sam's grandmother had died a few years prior, and he had successfully repressed his sexuality for several years out of deference to her and the faith that would reunite them. He spent the next day thinking on cosmic consequences. He worried that he had foolishly traded an eternity with her for a cheap thrill with an old lech. He worried if a moment's weakness would cost him indefinitely.

Meanwhile, Sam's mortal life continued. His grandfather still smoked his morning cigarette out of the window of their apartment and sipped his coffee, silently now that he was missing half of himself. Sam wanted to apologise to

Wassim for destroying their family's future — for losing his grandmother forever. But he could not. More than people in the so-called West, it seemed to Sam, Egyptians of every faith fast and afflict the soul with fervour to repent. Suffering was good, he thought — It was all he had to show for himself. Whatever gnawing guilt spun like a coffee grinder in his throat, it was always almost punishment enough for having done something his religion plainly forbade.

Sam had been raised well. Unlike Tony, Sam's grandparents were solid and capable, since they had already raised a child. Unlike Tony, Sam never once worried that his grandparents didn't know what they were doing. And yet it did happen on occasion that they made mistakes. For instance, one night, after Shabbat, on the subway ride home, Wassim instructed Little Sam to say ' إن شاء الله ' - InshAllah - Heavens-willing after Little Sam said he was excited to go to Luna Park at Coney Island with his grandparents the following Sunday.

'You never know what will happen,' Wassim said.

'But we are going? You said,' Sam said.

'Yes, روحي (- rouhi - my soul), but nothing in life is certain.'

'What do you mean?'

'I can die at any moment,' Wassim said. 'I'm not planning on it, don't be frightened! But it could happen, rouhi. And you have to be ready for it. Heavens-willing, I will live a very long life. We will all die eventually. And we are all in Heaven's hands, always. For everything.'

Decades later, and long after Wassim had died, everything Sam did was coloured by this. He went to grad school immediately after he got his bachelors. When he booked

114

travel, it was always only a few weeks ahead. His constitutional impatience served him well in journalism. He reported and wrote quick-hit news at lightning speed. But unlike genuinely talented journalists, he wrote this way not for its own sake but out of fear. Sam forever feared, Heaven-forbid, that he would die before saying his piece.

Another unforeseen result of Wassim's view of *Heavens-willing* was that, on occasion, Sam hurried along his relationships with men. Eventually, Sam became alright with sleeping around. And then his impatience meant that the sex, which should take however long it's going to take, became a biological chore to complete with haste. He impatiently awaited old age, when his sexuality would become irrelevant to the world and to himself. After a long day in the newsroom, he kissed Wassim on the forehead in his bed, retired to his room, and laid himself down, like a stiff, little corpse, arms at his sides.

19. The Temple الكنيس

'Hurry up, girls, or the service will finish before we arrive,' Lilia told Sam(a) and Ghozala as she walked, a few paces ahead of them.

'What's the rush?' Ghozala said.

'What's the point of going if we end up having to turn right back?' Lilia replied.

'Where are Wassim and your father?' Sam(a) asked.

'They're at the temple already, with grandfather,' Lilia said.

'Hawa doesn't come to temple?' Sam(a) asked.

'She stays home to make dinner,' Lilia said.

'What are we eating?' Sam(a) asked.

Lilia smiled. 'Of course, fish kofta, silly girl,' she said. 'You're in for a treat; it's her best dish.'

In New York, Sam(a) and Wassim ate the same Shabbat dinner almost every week: white fish kofta, breaded and browned, simmered in tomato sauce with cumin. A staple of the Egyptian Shabbat table.

Rushing along Luxor Street, Sam(a) saw a large, stately synagogue with a plaque in Arabic reading كنيس الياهو حزان - Eliyahou Hazan Synagogue.

'That's not it?' Sam(a) asked.

'No,' Lilia said. 'That's not our congregation.'

'It's right by your house. Isn't it easier to go there?' Sam(a) asked.

116

'Maybe in Mansoura it's different. Here, there are Jewish immigrants from all over the world, like there are non-Jewish Greeks and Armenians and Italians who have their different churches. There are different synagogues for different congregations. Our synagogue is a bit farther away.'

'What is your congregation?' Sam(a) asked.

'You and your questions — enough! I'm not a rabbi or a historian. I'm late and you're making me crazy,' Lilia said, punctuating her exasperation with a well-meaning smile.

A tangerine-tinted late afternoon, ethereal and honeyed, illuminated the Alexandrian coast as the Saadoun girls rushed through the streets. Sam(a) reckoned that at that hour, the essence of the shimmering gold platelets of the Mediterranean reflected across the entire city, permeating it, like a holy spirit — the Shabbat bride, as the Sabbath is known in the poetry of Jewish liturgy. Past several large parks and cafes turning to bars where people took apéritifs and smoked was a quiet residential street. Tucked away between stately homes with European edifices was a rectangular building in a more endemic style, with a flat roof. A large Star of David with geometric flourishes was chiseled into its forehead.

The synagogue was surrounded by a gate made of metal bars and cinderblocks. The Saadoun women passed through the open gate at the front. From the exterior of the synagogue, through an entryway, Sam(a) could see a foyer with a large bouquet of flowers, donated by one of the congregants. A muffled chanting noise rang forth from the prayer hall, past the foyer and a large set of closed doors. It was a warm sound, like Oum Kalthoum's raspy, full-bodied singing from the chest. Sam(a) felt as though past those doors was something like Heaven, at once familiar and exalted. Transfixed, a magnetic pull drew her toward the prayer hall, until Lilia grabbed her by the arm.

'This way,' Lilia said. 'That's the men's entrance.'

Lilia and Ghozala scurried around the side of the large, rectangular building, through a narrow alleyway between a grey cinderblock wall around the synagogue's perimeter and the building's exterior, made of a yellowed stone. On the side of the synagogue, there was a single metal door, made a little more presentable with a tapestry of black filigree. This entrance led directly to the back of the prayer hall, separated from its front by wooden barriers. The women, who sat in three rows of chairs at the back, could stand to see the service through latticework Stars of David carved into the wooden barriers. Sam(a) looked into the hall. There was a wooden

בימה - bima - pulpit at the centre of the room, a platform with low walls on each side, like a little cubicle. On either side of the pulpit were chandeliers with several rings of lightbulbs. And beside those chandeliers were a set of five Moorish multi-foil columns with little geometric flourishes. Below the arches formed by the columns were rows of wooden pews constructed in dark cherrywood, seats separated by armrests. At the very fore of the synagogue was a set of three marble steps leading to the Torah ark, hidden behind a maroon tapestry with benedictions embroidered in golden thread. On the elevated platform, together with the Torah ark, were men in regalia immediately identifiable as the clergy — the rabbi and the cantor. At the base of the steps and to their left was a pew facing the rest of the congregation. On one side of that pew were men dressed in fine suits. On the other end were very old men wearing galabeyas with sashes and tarboushes. The rest of the congregation wore Western-style suits, kippot head coverings, and tarboushes with fine suits. The smell of musks, after shave, and hair product mingled with the body heat of the crowded hall. There was no air-conditioning. The sound was like the chants of Tibetan lamas reading sutras. Deep, monotonous.

At the back of the synagogue, in the women's section, one or two women held prayerbooks and seemed to follow the service. The rest fanned themselves, sat in boredom — looking thoroughly miserable, chatted with their neighbours, or minded their children, who on occasion would become rowdy and inspire wide-eyed matronly admonition. Sam(a) wore a simple black dress, buttoned to the base of her neck, with a puffed skirt and three-quarter-length sleeves. Lilia wore a deep blue frock with long sleeves, and Ghozala wore a deep emerald dress with relatively the same dimensions. The three wore their hair tied back tightly into a chignon. The rest of the women in attendance wore brightly coloured and patterned dresses that were modest but that showed, for instance, the clavicles, beneath shawls that they would remove away from the synagogue. Their hair hung in tight curls or was straightened with hot combs and sculpted into waves, peaks, and tunnels.

'Where is your family?' Sam(a) whispered, as the Saadoun ladies shuffled past several seated women to some empty seats.

'Our grandfather Adam is at the head of the synagogue with the old-timers and the big donors,' Lilia said, pointing to him through the latticework. Adam wore a galabeya cloak.

His tarboush-clad head tilted over a prayerbook. He looked as though he was half-asleep, probably because of the mix of heat and the meditative humming of the congregation's collective chants.

'And there are my father and brother,' Lilia said, pointing somewhere to the left side of the congregation. They were indistinguishable in a sea of black hair, kippot, and tarboushes.

An older woman handed Lilia a copy of a prayerbook. Lilia opened it and bowed her head, closing her eyes. Sam(a) and Ghozala observed her. Ghozala smiled. Sam(a)'s grandmother in New York did not know how to read Hebrew either. Wassim only knew how to read the sounds of the Hebrew alphabet without understanding it.

Ten minutes later, Sam(a) felt she as if was going to faint. Between the form-fitting frock, and all of the scent and body heat swirling about the room, she worried her head would explode.

'Would it be alright if I stepped outside for some air?' Sam(a) asked Lilia and Ghozala. Lilia looked up from her prayerbook, still open to the same page, and inspected Sam(a) disapprovingly.

'Of course,' Ghozala said, preempting Lilia's disapproval. 'It's very hot in here.' There was a small twitch in Ghozala's left eye that caught Sam(a)'s attention. Perhaps it was her perspiration creeping into the corners of her eyes or the smell of the congregations colognes irritating them, Sam(a) thought. She shot Ghozala a wide, thankful smile, shot up and glided past other women and children, all moistened by the ambience of a crowded house on Shabbat. In Ancient Egypt, such women wore cones of perfumed wax atop their heads, so that the vapours of a sweltering evening could be made more sweet-smelling. Sam(a) enjoyed this useless trivia in her New York City public school system history lessons. But she realised, actually in Egypt and in practice, that the combination of heat and scent that the Egyptians seemed to have enjoyed since time immemorial was suffocating her.

A couple of women, both wearing low heels and shawls, strolled slowly, arm-in-arm, returning from the back of the building to the women's side entrance. Sam(a) felt that her safest bet in all things womanhood, 1930s Alexandria, and her family's experience of faith was imitation. So she strolled slowly, arms behind her back, toward the back of the building. As they approached, the couple of women whispered to each other and giggled. Sam(a) worried that something about her comportment or her dress or her femininity or her Egyptianness or her Judaism or her hair or her shoes was amiss, and yet neither of the approaching women looked at her at all. Sam(a) was not the source of their amusement.

Sam(a) turned the corner, and behind the synagogue, she found a narrow space, dimly lit by a single flood light. In the dusk, the pale orange of the light set on faces and stones like a resin. At the far corner of the back wall was a single door, without the black filagree of the women's side entrance — just an unceremonious, unvarnished metal door that led to a backroom, and past that, to the side entrance of the men's portion of the prayer hall. It became clear to Sam(a) almost immediately what this space had been: a singular venue for members of the opposite sex from pious families to encounter each other. Sam(a) counted 20 or so people behind the synagogue. Women stood up against the back of synagogue and the wall across from it. The young men stood at the centre of the alley.

The few young people of the alley who had not yet found a conversation partner of the opposite sex had a same-sex friend, like the two women she had seen coming from the alley. A wingman bodyguard. Sam(a) wondered if this was due to shyness or a need to have a witness at hand to confirm that nothing untoward had happened. Sam(a) had no one.

Sam(a) stood with her back against the wall of the synagogue. And then, feeling uncomfortable with that, she switched to the opposite side and hung herself like a painting on the cinderblock wall of the synagogue's perimeter. She waited. She put her arms behind her back in a way that forced her into good posture and more protruding breasts. No men looked at her. So she slouched and looked down at her little, black ballet flats.

She wondered if she was ugly. She felt guilty — physically nauseous in the pit of her stomach, for not having been better looking. She was uncertain what constituted beauty to the people engaged in the sort of waltz around her. Should her breasts have been bigger? She recalled a high school friend who dressed as a flapper for Halloween say that in the 1920s, European and American women downplayed the size of their breasts. What about in 1930s Alexandria? And was Sam(a) too brown or not brown enough? Probably too brown, if anything. As a child, Wassim would tell his grandson not to play too long in the sun, lest he become dark-skinned. And Wassim would recall that his own father had told his sister Ghozala, the darker of his two sisters, to apply yogurt to her face to make herself more pale and marriageable. *Why should*

*I feel guilty for being ugly, whatever ugliness is to these people? Sam(a)
thought. They're all going to end up someone's grandparents. They're
all going to need to leave this place in a panic sometime over the next
30 or 40 years, and then this alleyway will be empty, and none of my
feelings will have mattered.* And then she began to pity them.
She wondered — If they had known that everything would
end in just a few years, would they shoehorn their romance
and lust into such clandestine little spaces? Or would it live
out in the streets, like in Almodovar's Movida? And which
was better — the puritanical hypocrisy of 1930s Alexandria,
or the sloppy sexual liberation of Spain after fascism that
Sam(a) as Sam had always admired from afar?

'What are you thinking about, young miss?' a disembodied
voice asked.

Sam(a) looked up. Not very much taller than she was a
smiling man with a square jaw and a diastema, like Omar
Sharif's and Dakota Johnson's — a small vacation between
his two front teeth. His eyebrows were very close friends.
Atop his head was a profusion of lustrous, dark natural hair
— like the unshorn wool of a black sheep. Other men Sam(a)
had seen in this world had the habit of suppressing their hair
to the skull. His hair was more unkempt than any she had
seen in 1930s Alexandria.

'Why so sullen?' he continued.

'Not sullen, just in my feelings,' Sam(a) said.

'Inside of your feelings— What a poetic turn of phrase,'
he said.

Sam(a) wondered if she continued to employ 21st century
colloquialisms in 1930s Alexandria, if she would become the
Sylvia Plath of this society.

'I'm Antoine,' he said. Sam(a) looked at him.

'Antoun,' he clarified. 'Antoun Daoudi son of Haroun and Rachelle.'

'Sam(a) — It's a pleasure,' she said.

'I haven't seen you here before,' he asked.

'I'm from Mansoura,' she said, hoping he wouldn't ask her about Mansoura. 'Apparently.'

Antoun chuckled. 'Lovely,' he said, approaching Sam(a). He placed his hand on the cinderblock just above her shoulder. This excited her.

Where would they go? Sam(a) wondered. She wondered if she should say something forward to hurry things along. *Or would that scare this kind of man away?* She looked down at their shoes. His feet were so grotesquely large, next to hers.

'There's something unusual about you,' he said, nudging her chin and her gaze back toward him with his index finger. Antoun's touch startled Sam(a). She was certain that a man of this generation would be careful not to touch a woman of the opposite sex to whom he was not related. None of the other couples in the alley touched each other. They spoke inaudible, horny, poetic words. But there was never so much as a handshake between them. They were forced into discretion and creativity.

Sam(a) looked into his eyes. All she found was the reflection of the flood light from above. She waited for him to continue.

'Something unlike all these other girls,' he continued.

She felt uncomfortable, suddenly. She wondered for a moment if he had sensed somehow that despite what she had by then made certain was a vagina, she was also — somewhere else, and perhaps there too — a man. Had he

124

been attracted to her manhood? Was he gay? Or were all the genteel, bourgeois men of his generation the sort of soft-spoken dandies whom Sam(a) thought to be latently gay in the modern-day — that is to say, a few decades later?

'And yet I feel as though I know you, Sama the Mansoureya,' he said, in a strange sort of trance. 'Intimately.'

20. Joy of All Who Sorrow
Всех скорбящих Радость

'I'm afraid everything's closing, Tony,' I said. 'We should have started earlier. Or I should've met you earlier.'

We were fast approaching Brighton Beach Avenue's end — or start, coming from Coney Island. The little that was left to see of the street was emptying of its life. Its inhabitants and their commerce in souvenirs and Soviet soul food were disappearing. I knew Brighton Beach to close early, but this particular End of Business felt sudden. Brighton had deserted me. I know it sounds ridiculous, but the street had suddenly emptied to such an astounding degree that it felt as though all of the neighbourhood was in on it. All of a sudden, they had all decided to get lost.

A line of an old song called زوروني - *Zourouni* - *Visit Me* came to mind — حرام تنسونى بالمرة - *Don't forget me all of a sudden*. One of our Alexandrian important people wrote that. Maybe the Alexandrians are especially afraid to be forgotten. And maybe that is not a pitiful but a powerful fear. English-language historians describe societies preoccupied with mourning and matters of the afterlife as sophisticated. Mournfulness is interpreted by Western academia a sign that those societies had progressed past concerns of mere survival — hunting, gathering, and shelter. Seen from another vantage point, those societies had become bourgeois and soft enough to be wistful.

Shut the fuck up, you fucking cry baby. You're running out of time.

We moved from block to block at vertiginous speeds. Tony matched my pace. It felt as though we were facing a dead end. There was a stillness that reinforced the chill of an evening by the ocean. That chill grasped me by the throat.

'What about your gay app?' Tony asked. Anything?'

'A few guys. No one I'd be down for,' I said.

'We're just looking for someone to host and maybe watch us, right? Who cares who it is,' Tony said.

'Yeah, but South Brooklyn is the setting of a lot of NYC crime shows. We probably shouldn't go to just anyone's place,' I said. 'I don't want to end up chained to a radiator in someone's basement or chopped up in chunks and stuffed in a freezer.'

'Right,' Tony said.

We passed Güllüoglu Baklava. Couples sat over tea and plates of baklava and large, cubed Turkish delight.

'This is the finest baklava in New York City,' I said.

'Turkish? A bit misplaced, isn't it?' Tony observed.

'There are several Turkish businesses here — This one, another restaurant, a grocer. I thought at first maybe it's because there are many Post-Soviet Central Asian people who live and work here, and they seem to view Turkey with a feeling of kinship and cultural reverence. But then I Googled the Russia connection, and it turns out that throughout history, the Ottoman and Russian empires engaged in turf wars. I find it amusing that the Turkish Americans carved out a place for themselves here,' I said.

'You've given so much thought to this place,' Tony said.

'Do you want some cake, Tony?' I asked. I'd have gladly

paid everything in my wallet to fill his loose lips with sweets.

'I've had enough food for one night,' he replied. 'I'm probably already too bloated for you to see me naked.'

I searched the streets for signs of life — for some attraction other than Russian and Russian-adjacent foods.

'You're beautiful, I'm sure,' I said, in a tone approaching enthusiasm.

'Have you ever seen Russia, or thought of going on a trip there?' he asked. 'Russia Russia. Not whatever Russia in the 90s this is meant to be.'

A flash of light caught the corner of my eye and drew it up a side street with homes smaller than the large Soviet-style buildings closer to the water. From a distance, I saw one flicker of candlelight floating on a dark street. That flame seemed to birth another and another, until there was a small constellation of them. On occasion they would go out with a gust of wind and then reappear, moments later. I took Tony's hand. He hesitated for a half-second. I relaxed my grasp of his hand. I would have let him go and ventured alone toward the constellation of lights if he would not follow. But then he laced his fingers into mine more resolutely. When he did that, I felt something in my chest resembling feelings for him. I recalled suddenly that I had felt similar feelings in my chest for other men several times. Must have been dozens of times in just three decades of life, one of which I had spent out of the closet. I recalled what came of those feelings.

As we approached, it became clear that our destination was a crowded place of worship in a private home. Some of the believers queued up to enter the house. Others poured out of the home-church into the street and congregated there, holding taper candles poked through styrofoam cups to shield their flames from the wind. As we walked toward the house, I felt some strange energy travel between our palms, like I was sharing a bit of my electrons or my soul with him. I wondered if I was losing a bit of myself in whatever transaction transpired between our palms. In scientific reality, it was probably only a bit of our perspiration, mingling. Approaching the house, I stiffened my fingers until they lost him in their mock rigour mortis. When he was gone from my body, I felt relieved not to have had to tell him that I would feel disrespectful holding his hand in such a place. I did not dare look him in the face to see how he reacted to my cowardice. Maybe my cowardice was respectful. Or maybe multiple realities live side-by-side. Maybe Tony felt the way I did about holding hands at the church: that there was no point angering a congregation of Russian Orthodox people in their place of worship.

The queue moved quickly through a driveway, curled around to a back door and up a small set of cement stairs, through a backroom and into what was once a home's den. The line made its way through a hall of saints with furrowed brows cast in metallic, hot colours. Their deep-set, sagacious and life-worn, almond-shaped eyes bore into us. We were trespassers in their house. The saints intermittently touched their hearts or lifted a hand — either askance or offering us absolution and refuge in faith. Their eyes seemed to follow us as we passed. All around the den, planted across the room's hardwood floors at key locations beside the saint icons were bouquets of white flowers and stands holding spirals of candles. At the very centre of the den, on an elevated platform, was an icon of the Virgin Mary wearing a large crown, the shape of the dome on a Russian Orthodox church. She wore a red cape with a cap that sat under her crown and a gown with the ornamentation of traditional Russian village folk clothing — the kind that the mannequins wore in the window at Anadyr Art & Souvenir. In her arms, and wearing a smaller crown and matching outfit was the Baby Jesus, sitting upright — knowing, adult eyes anticipating the events that the faithful were commemorating in that house at Brighton Beach, two millennia and two decades later. The Virgin and Child were surrounded by the Apostles and other holy figures. This icon received the most attention and the most candles. Several older women wearing babushkas over the most formal and fanciful of the clothes available at the bargain basement shops on Brighton Beach Avenue stood before the icon, deep in prayer.

I stole a glance of Tony in the candlelight. The pale orange glow of the flames had set on him like a resin, underlining his features. He looked like a saint — pensive brow. He was beautiful. But then I saw him look at me. He had probably felt my eyes on him, in him. I looked away. He had mostly seen me in the dusk and dark. I was certain that with my face illuminated by all the candles, he would find me disgusting — discover the blemishes just under the epidermis that make known that I am probably more than a little unhealthy and unbecoming. He looked at me. And then he looked away, in deference to the Virgin of the house-church and her Child.

A woman approached us from behind. She was a zaftig and middle aged. Her hair was golden with highlights. She wore heavy makeup, a white dress, and leggings. She had

130

been standing in a corner of the room, and she had evidently been observing us observing each other. She patted me on the shoulder. I first noticed her long, pink acrylic nails. She gestured for us to follow her outside. I felt my heart sink into my stomach.

She escorted us to the front yard, where a large wooden fold-out table had baskets filled with identical sets of grocery items. There were the kulich cakes from before, some with a single candle planted in them, eggs wrapped with plastic images of ornate Russian folk scenes, and boxes of salt.

'What's this?' Tony asked.

The woman laughed to indicate she was shy about her English, and that he would perhaps not understand her over the din of the faithful exchanging greetings and reminders that 'Он воскрес' - On voskryes - He is Risen.

'This is a church,' she said. 'Joy of All Who Sorrow. It's the church name.'

'I see. And what are these baskets?' he asked.

She thought for a moment. 'Symbols,' she said. 'Symbols of our Easter.' She motioned for them to wait. It is the same hand gesture in the Middle East, North Africa, and Russia — a thumb touched to the index and middle fingers. She rifled through some of the baskets, retrieved two small kulich cakes, put them in a plastic bag, and handed it to me.

'Thank you so much,' I said. 'How much are they?'

'It's a gift, boys — good boys,' she said. 'From our church. It means a new life. New life in Christ.'

We thanked her for her generosity and disappeared back into the night, away from the flickering candles and their reflections on the asphalt of the street.

'There's no such thing as a free lunch,' I said, as we ambled away from the church.

Tony said nothing. I was fed-up with myself too. I wanted Tony to take my hand. But that was a moment that had come and passed before we entered the church, and I was not about to take his. I wanted him to reach out for me. I wanted him to sweep me up in his arms and refuse to leave, even if my hand stiffened up eventually or one or both of us had to die. We would be as two petrified trees in Southern Brooklyn.

Tony looked ahead to the electric light from the subway overpass back on Brighton Beach Avenue. When we returned there, we discovered it had become even more desolate and still than before.

21. Waiting Room غرفة الانتظار

Sam(a) ate great, big mouthfuls of bread-crusted fish kofta in a tomato and cumin broth. One only feels their mouth full and actively tastes a morsel of food for seconds at a time; that's science. But Sam(a) was resolved to change this — to feel herself to be completely immersed in a state of taste — of culinary rapture for the whole duration of her Shabbat meal.

In New York, Sam(a) had used Japanese パン粉 - panko - breadcrumbs to bread the Shabbat fish kofta dinners that she prepared for herself and her grandfather. She gave the otherwise light-flavoured tomato-cumin broth a kick with sriracha. The Egyptian version of fish kofta — which is a bit like saying the Italian version of pizza or the Arab version of hummus — was not at all spicy, but beyond that, the flavour was entirely different. Sam(a) reckoned it was the purity of the tomatoes, free of GMOs. She felt herself to never have tasted a tomato before. It was as though — at least judging by the tomatoes — her time in New York had been only a faint aftertaste of living.

'Easy, girl. Do you have someplace else to be?' Lilia asked. Sam(a) looked up, embarrassed.

'Let her eat her meal in peace, for Heaven's sake. Always a word to say,' Hawa told Lilia. 'She has an appetite like a man, our Sama!' Hawa added. Hawa looked at Sam(a) with a proud smile. Sam(a) looked at Hawa, wondering how much she knew and how she knew it.

'Ghozala, my daughter, give her rice — The girl has no rice, poor thing!' Hawa continued.

'I'm sorry. I don't eat rice,' Sam(a) said.

Hawa looked at Sam(a) with a blank stare, mouth agape.

'Are you one of the Moroccan girls? You eat stew with the semolina?' Lilia asked.

'Don't pry into her life. Let her eat,' Hawa insisted.

'I just don't want to get fat, so I eat less bread and starches,' Sam(a) told Lilia.

'All of the children today are like this. Insane,' Adam said. This had been the first time Sam(a)'s stern, galabeya-clad great-great-grandfather ever verbally acknowledged her existence. She was relieved that he saw her. Sam(a) was uncertain of the rules of science in this alternate reality. In that moment, she discovered Adam to be a man of few words. Sam(a) wondered if it was perhaps because of religiosity that he avoided speaking to or looking at young women whom he thought to be non-relatives.

'Ghozala, my love, give Sama her rice,' Hawa said. 'Sama, my dear, listen to me: Eat the rice with the kofta, together. Without the rice, the kofta is too salty. My rice has almost no fat. Very healthy.'

Sam(a) nodded in defeat. Ghozala, who had been sitting beside Sam(a), held out her hand for Sam(a)'s plate. When Ghozala returned Sam(a)'s plate with a large pile of glistening rice, Sam(a) nodded to thank her and noticed that Ghozala still had a twitch in her left eye, like Doctor Fahmy back in Brooklyn. Sam(a) returned to her koftas and her thoughts.

Eye twitches are common, Sam(a) thought — Many people who drink too much coffee or smoke or experience anxiety have eye-twitches. Sam(a) piled rice onto her fork, then turned to look at Ghozala once more and found that Ghozala had been silently staring at Sam(a). Ghozala smiled politely and returned to her fish kofta.

The entire room was suddenly jolted by music playing from a phonograph in the adjacent sitting room. Wassim who had excused himself moments earlier came striding into the room, shoulders back, like a triumphant soldier returning from battle.

'God forgive you, my son,' Ayoub told him, shaking his head. 'What have I told you about playing the phonograph on Shabbat?'

'The heart wants what it wants!' Wassim declared, in heavily accented English.

Adam, who had his mouth full, muttered under his breath, upset. Finally, he exploded: 'We can't understand our own children anymore, for Heaven's sake!'

'Look at you! You've upset grandfather to play one of your stupid records!' Lilia said. 'Are you happy? At least you could have played my Chopin or Charles Trenet — something refined.'

'This is the highest art, I'll have you know — from Abdel Wahab's latest picture يحيا الحب - Long live love,' Wassim replied, as if these details would make a difference.

'Who is this woman singing?' Sam(a) asked.

'Leila Mourad, of course. The song is يا ما ارق النسيم - *Oh How Sweet the Wind*. A fire song, no?' Wassim said. Sam(a) nodded and returned to her rice, on the verge of laughter.

'It's fire' would again become a slang expression for Wassim's heartfelt enthusiasm decades later, in English, in the United States.

'Anyway, grandfather smokes in bed all day on Saturdays,' Wassim continued. 'You can see the smoke coming out from the bottom of the door to their little apartment.' Adam looked at Wassim with simmering disdain. In New York, Wassim would forbid his grandson from work on Shabbat. But despite the Shabbat prohibition on electricity, they would turn on the lights as needed and watch television.

'Your grandfather smokes from a shisha pipe that your grandmother prepares,' Ayoub said. 'And what he does is none of your business; it's between him and Heaven.' Sam(a) wondered if Ayoub had meant that Hawa prepared the pipe before Shabbat or that she was made to break her own observance of Shabbat to serve her husband tobacco. As a child in Brooklyn, Sam(a) would turn on the stove for Wassim, because as Wassim put it, Sam(a) would have more time to repent. Sam(a) imagined that Hawa was no more than a decade younger than Adam.

'Why should I be forbidden from enjoying Shabbat with music?' Wassim said. 'After a long week of work, this is my only chance to rest! Shabbat is for rest!'

'In the old days, we sang on Shabbat!' Hawa declared, smiling.

'And then Moses led the Hebrews through the Red Sea,' Wassim said.

Hawa burst into laughter. And with that, the children broke into laughter. Adam continued to eat, unfazed or unaware.

Ayoub continued to look at Wassim with enraged eyes, until finally he returned to his plate of fish kofta and rice. The music continued to play.

Ayoub put down his fork and knife. 'I have to speak with you — with the girls,' he said.

Sam(a) stopped eating and looked at Ayoub.

'Girls, you are not to go out after dark, and you are never to go out alone , even in the daytime,' he said.

'Of course we wouldn't,' Lilia said, overzealous and anxious, as usual. 'Why do you say this now?'

'I didn't want to alarm you, but if you must know: I've read several stories in the paper of missing women,' he said. 'All from Cleopatra-Sidi Gaber. It's a pattern.'

'My colleague told me about this at work,' Wassim said. 'Disappearing women. Gone without a trace. The perfect crime, they say.'

How sweet we were! Sam(a) thought, as she ate. She imagined that for the Saadouns and the rest of Alexandria, before the great catastrophes of the 20th century, a couple of missing persons was cause for great alarm. In the U.S., such things wouldn't have made the news unless the missing women were especially rich, white, or photogenic. But then, emerging from her smugness and her supper, Sam(a) recalled Antoun from the temple that evening and Tiresias from Ancient Greece. Freshly confined to the home, Sam(a) couldn't immediately identify a way to sleep with Antoun before she was jolted back into Brooklyn in the 21st century. Sam(a) thought about the closed port that was her family's house on Flower Street. She felt a familiar constriction inside — in her lungs, a shortness of breath. A narrow, like the tight space between the synagogue and the cinderblock and metal gate around its perimeter.

Sam(a) looked at Hawa, who had finished what little she had served herself of the meal she prepared for the Saadouns. Hawa looked into the distance at something unseen. Perhaps Hawa was resting her eyes on something before her, or maybe her sight had retreated inside or backward to a more deep-set past. *What sort of past does Hawa have?* Sam(a) wondered —*How did she manage to pass all the time from youth to old age? By singing a cappella folk songs? Surely she felt the same boredom and anxiety that I had in my youth? Did she swallow it?*

Sam(a) saw Hawa in her mind's eye, wandering about the back yard where the family's newer generations had tucked her away with her husband. She saw Hawa endlessly pacing to-and-fro like life was an open-air waiting room. And perhaps it was, for such pious people.

Sam(a) gasped for air in a familiar way, something between a yawn and a sigh.

22. Freedom Street 01000110
01110010 01100101 01100101
01100100 01101111 01101101
00100000 01010011 01110100
01110010 01100101 01100101
01110100 00100000

There were signs of life back on the Brighton Beach boardwalk. Brighton Beach Avenue was entirely quiet, but on the boardwalk, husbands and wives strolled to-and-fro. They wore down coats from the bargain basement shops on Brighton Beach Avenue. They delighted in the stillness of the night — engaging in a European mode of relaxation called la dolce far niente - sweet inertia. To my anxious Egyptian eyes, they looked like zombies.

They say that the boardwalk at Brighton Beach looks like St. Petersburg. Some of the night people of the boardwalk looked like their parents had, strolling in their sensible, Soviet, monochromatic woollens along the frigid Baltic.

I was hurriedly scrolling through my options on Pound while Tony observed the passersby. Wassim had always marvelled at how quickly I texted — how fast my thumbs were able to move. Wassim's last mobile was a flip phone with no internet connectivity. He was not a luddite. He had seen many fads come and go, and he was keen to learn new things. He was learning Mandarin when he died. But something about the way I had become drawn into my phone, the way my head bent before it, upset him. Wassim's hatred of smartphones was not a question of the privacy concerns that people raise these days. Wassim was not the kind of man who cared whether online marketers knew he loved oatmeal. And yet he was certain that each new generation of smart phone was a kind of progress that takes a step backward.

'What about this guy?' I asked Tony, showing him my phone. 'He's in Sheepshead Bay — just one stop away on the Q train.' His username was an emoji: a pair of suspicious-looking side-eyes. In Pound parlance, this meant that this Pound user was 'looking' - that he was actively seeking a hook-up. His profile picture showed him standing on the beach covered head-to-toe in Adidas athletic wear. He had cropped his head out of the picture. He was 41 years old, 177 centimetres tall, 67 kilos, 'Average' body type, male, discreet, single, HIV negative on PrEP, and looking for casual hook-ups.

'What's his face look like?' Tony asked.

'I thought you didn't care,' I replied. 'This guy says he'd be down just to watch.'

'Well I don't want him to look scary,' Tony said. 'It'd be a bit distracting to have a Picasso leering at us at the end of the bed, don't you think?'

I asked for a face pic. The Pound user blocked me immediately, in response.

'The little gonad blocked me!' I exclaimed. 'Can you believe? The nerve of some people!'

Another account appeared on the menu grid of possibilities. Just 1.3 miles away. Blank profile. 'HOST' was his username. No stats. Just a few more-or-less words in the self-description: 'STR8 4 STR8.'

Hey bro, I wrote. *What's up?*

Faggot, HOST replied.

The fuck? We're both on Pound fuck face? I replied.
What a sad, faceless little man. If you had any balls you'd show your sorry little face when you use homophobic slurs on a gay sex app.

Tell me that to my face, HOST replied.

I would if you had one!

I'll slice you

I reported and blocked the profile.

'What's wrong,' Tony said. 'You look upset.'

'Nothing — just a whimsical, little Coney Island crackhead said he wanted to slice me up!'

'Ah the goodly people of the hook-up app, society's cream of the crop,' Tony said and returned to his people watching.

A yellow sports car pulled up to the roundabout near the bench where we sat. A pale blue and purple strobe light turned on inside the car. The driver rolled down the window and the song *Плачу на техно - Plachu na Tyekna — Crying over Techno* played with heavy bass from his surround sound. Tony and I watched him look out his window broodingly into the infinite blackness of the Atlantic Ocean for a moment. Then the song ended. He flicked a cigarette out the window and drove off into the night.

I looked back to my phone. I had several messages —
not on Pound but on Instagram. It was Akram, my digital
friend in Alexandria.

Hey Sam

Good morning

Or goodnight, whatever.

I have a surprise for you, Akram wrote. *I spoke with a municipal
history expert at the Bibliotecha Alexandrina, our famous library.*

My heart began to beat through my chest.

Flower Street is now called Freedom Street.

*I went there to take you some photos, so you could finally see it. One
moment.*

And then they came to me like a dam had broken, in
rapid succession — photos of Freedom Street. I reckoned
not much had changed since Wassim's time. The building
were just as regal. They had only become a bit more
ghostly, beaten about by the elements and cloaked in a
film of age. Then Akram sent two videos: one of the large
coastal avenues and the glistening Mediterranean beyond
them and the second of young Akram walking up Freedom
Street. At the head of the street, close to the water, was a
Chili's - تشيليز - one of the American chain restaurants
famous for the barbecue ribs. I marvelled at the sight of an
American restaurant on a side street off the Alexandrian
coast. I was both relieved and disturbed to find something
so familiar there. And then I realised that this — seeing
Wassim's street after a lifetime of wondering — was a
heavy undertaking. What if nothing beyond the old-looking
buildings and the Chili's was familiar to me? If Flower
Street felt as foreign as New York, perhaps the problem of

my constant sorrow lied with me and not my displacement.

'Notice there are some shops here that still call themselves Flower, the old street name,' Akram said in the video, in English. Tony was startled by the sudden high-volume static sound from the video. It was the sound of the winds from the Mediterranean assaulting Akram's phone as punishment for capturing and transferring to me what I should only have again if I actually made it there. 'Here's a battery shop — Flower Street Batteries,' Akram continued. 'And a little cigarette shop — 'Flower Tobacconist.'

I thought about the still-living people of Flower Street. Freedom in Arabic — حرية - horiya — is just as sweet-sounding a word as flowers — زهرة - zahra. And yet there was evidently something about modern Egyptian people that would hang onto the old, colonial-era name. Maybe, seen from another vantage point, their nostalgia was not self-defeating and sad. Maybe Egyptians are culturally — and as a function of the culture of Islam and of Egypt's history with famine, epidemics, and other periods of los and want — opposed to waste. Maybe there are several simultaneous realities.

'This is it,' Akram said. Our house on Flower Street had become a small apartment building. I wondered if our building had been bulldozed or just updated or expanded to accommodate several, separate quarters. We had no old photos of the house, growing up — only photos from up the street. Then, Akram continued inland from the sea, southward toward Borg el Arab. I saw an alley beside the building where we had lived. I felt as though I had seen the alley in a dream. I tried to zoom in on it with my thumb and index finger, but the video became too grainy to inspect it further. I flipped through the accompanying photos. There it was — an alleyway just beside the apartment building, and over it stood a marble archway decorated with a relief of three oversized jasmine buds, interwoven with ribbon, sitting atop two Grecian pillars. I looked up into the ocean ahead of me. I wondered if I flung myself into the Atlantic, if I would wash up on Freedom Street, beneath this archway, and be buried there by someone like Akram, who would be Egyptian enough to understand why I had come.

'You're crying, Sam,' Tony said.

'No, it's the ocean wind hitting my eyes,' I said.

'You're crying, Sam,' Tony insisted. 'Those are tears.'

'This is the street of my grandfather, who raised me,' I said, showing him my phone. A young man who is like him in some ways took these photos because he knows I've wanted to see it and couldn't.'

'Good man,' Tony said. It was a pleasure to hear Tony say something earnest after all his snark and skepticism about my religiosity, my plan to return, my adventures with hypnosis.

'It's a sort of goodness I haven't felt here in years,' I said. 'That's is why I'm going back. In Alexandria, people will know what I need, intuitively. My grandfather would have done this for someone in my situation, and his family too, Heaven rest them.'

'That's why you're going to mentally castrate yourself tomorrow morning,' Tony said. 'Religion is a hell of a drug.'

'God forgive you, Tony,' I said. 'Religion is the only thing keeping me alive until now.'

'Religion is why you won't give me more than one night,'

he said. 'Your last gay night.'

'That's not true,' I replied. 'I've given men like you more chances than I can count. I banked my soul on a gay Hollywood romance— a fiction I never found. And by doing that, I've taken myself farther from this street. The truth is, when this street, and your feelings, and my face crumble, there will still be the Heavens. And if I repent one day, before my death, I will rest my head there and be free from my sorrow.'

And solitude, I should have said. What a beautiful word — العزلة - elaozla - *Solitude*. The sound of it is like a void echoing from the back of the throat. Some American people name their children *Constance*, which is beautiful, no doubt. But I love the Catholic faithful of the Spanish-speaking world who dare to name their daughters something as true to life as the name *Soledad - Solitude*.

23. Hourglass الساعة الرملية

Ilyas the tailor had just 20 minutes available the following Monday to see Sam(a) for measurements. Ghozala and Lilia escorted Sam(a) to Monsieur Edouard's first thing in the morning only for Ilyas's helper Hani to turn them away once more, poking his little, moustachioed head through the scarlet velour drapes behind the shop door. The drapes and Hani were meant to hide female forms from the peeping Toms getting off the tram at Sidi Gaber. Hani instructed the girls to return at exactly 2:30 in the afternoon. 'Not a moment sooner, not a second later,' he said. 'We are a great deal busier than usual, and we don't want to keep you waiting,' Hani explained. And then he vanished behind his scarlet drapes.

On the way to Monsieur Edouard's, passing the flower shop of Flower Street, the worker who had offered Sam(a) a rosebud days before smiled and nodded at her as she passed. Lilia, who had been walking a few steps ahead of Sam(a) looked back at her for a second, eyes like daggers. Sam(a) looked down at her shoes. When Lilia turned away, just as the Saadoun girls turned the corner onto Tigran Basha, Sam(a) looked back at the shopkeeper, whose gaze followed her up the street. Sam(a) offered him a discreet wave of the hand. The shopkeeper shot her a beaming, earnest smile from the heart, fresh like the newest of his shop's roses. And then suddenly, feeling a bit shy, he continued with his task of sweeping wilted flower petals and dead, fallen leaves from his shop floor out into the gutter.

Ilyas used the back of his hand to pat the small of Sam(a)'s back in the way some people check to see if a pot on a stove is hot. A quick pat. He seemed to observe the jiggle of the negligible excess that she had in that space. He looked at her disapprovingly. Lilia was quite thin and Ilyas seemed uninterested in her. Ghozala had rounder hips and thick legs. On occasion, Ilyas turned his gaze from his measuring tape and Sam(a)'s insufficient thickness to give Ghozala a once-over. Ghozala blushed as she sat beside Lilia on a scarlet loveseat. The room was lit by a handful of Tiffany lamps with shades made of various hues of green glass and bronze bases. The light fell into the black fabric that hung about the walls of the room and gave it a nuance in the way that coffee very subtly flavours chocolate cake. Hani the helper placed a single, unshaded bronze lamp just below the pedestal where Sam(a) stood for her measurements. The light blinded her. It also served to enhance the shadows around Ilyas's face, like he was about to tell a campfire story. Ilyas had a narrow, long face with a prominent bone on the bridge of his nose.

'Can I offer you something, ladies,' Hani said. 'Coffee, cake?'

Hani was a short, squat man. In stark contrast to Ilyas, who was tall and thin. An Egyptian take on Laurel and Hardy .

'We've just had lunch, I'm afraid,' Lilia said. 'Thank you, Mister Hani.'

Hani nodded and scurried away behind the black cloth that surrounded the room. From the back room, Hani produced a candy dish with fine chocolates.

'Bonbons pour mesdames,' he said. 'Indulge yourselves, please.'

Ilyas's eyes focused on Sam(a)'s shoulders. His tape measure ran along the length of her back. This had been the first time a man had touched or been in close proximity to her. She felt as she had when Antoun placed his hand against the wall above her shoulder. Unlike Antoun, Ilyas was not terribly handsome, Sam(a) thought, but there was an intensity to his eyes. The charcoal-black of his lashes and brows, even in the strange lighting of the fitting room of Monsieur Edouard's, underlined the intensity of his focus. Sam(a) felt herself attracted to the passion of Ilyas's work.

'How generous,' Ghozala said, plucking up a dark chocolate bonbon, dusted with powdered cocoa. Lilia looked at Ghozala, perturbed, and then the chocolates with the same expression, but she also picked one of the sweets from the dish. They popped the sweets into their mouths.

'Tell your friends,' Ilyas said, still moving his tape measure about Sam(a)'s shoulders and on occasion calling numbers out to Hani, who noted them with a small pencil in a notepad.

'How is business, Mister Ilyas?' Lilia asked.

'Same as it's been for the past several years,' he said. 'Not quite what it used to be.'

'Ah yes, the economic crisis,' Lilia said.

'That and the competition,' Ilyas said, running the tape measure from Sam(a)'s hip to her ankle. Sam(a) felt only an index finger and thumb at two points on her waist and leg, and that was enough to pump up the volume on the stirring within her.

148

'Monsieur Edouard has given us a new shop in Sporting that we open only a few days a week, just five minutes away from here, but then he expanded further with another shop in Sporting and then another a little farther up the coast,' Ilyas continued. 'We're bleeding business. I tried to contact his business associates to tell them the man is competing with himself and driving the locals to ruin in the balance — They won't hear of it.'

'I'm very sorry, Mister Ilyas,' Lilia said. 'My brother works for a shipping company and says that with the new tariff scheme, we are now exporting more cotton to Europe and importing less goods, so let's hope things will improve, Heaven-willing.'

'Heaven-willing,' Ilyas responded unenthusiastically.

'The king is making great strides for us, Heaven help him,' Lilia said. 'And the Swiss are a cold-blooded people — It's known.'

'Monsieur Edouard is a British,' Ilyas said.

'Even worse!' Lilia said.

'We will insist that our friends in the neighbourhood come exclusively to Monsieur Edouard's,' Ghozala said, emphatically.

'That deserves another sweet,' Ilyas said. 'Hani.'

Hani ran to retrieve the dish of bonbons from an end table in the corner of the room. Just as Ghozala was about to take another, Lilia swiftly slapped her hand.

'Forgive us Hani, my sister is becoming too fat. No one will marry her,' Lilia said.

Sam(a) observed Ghozala's face — eyes rounded with embarrassment.

'Nonsense,' Ilyas said. 'Your sister has an hourglass shape that is very handsome indeed.'

'All the same,' Lilia said. 'Hourglasses are designed to run out of time, and so are we.'

Silent, Ghozala shook her head and raised a hand of thanks to Hani, who shrank back with the dish of sweets. Ghozala's eyes followed the chocolates to the back room in the way the flower shop keeper's eyes had followed Sam(a) up Flower Street.

'Can you believe the nerve!' Lilia said, moments later, as the girls bought حواويشي - hawawshi - minced lamb sandwiches on Tigran Basha. 'Feeding us bonbons so we get fat as houses and have to go back, get re-measured, and buy entirely new wardrobes! The cunning! And then there was Ghozala, the perfect dope, taking one bonbon after the other. I didn't even want the first!'

Ghozala put her eyes and soul in her hawawshi. Her eyebrows raised of their own accord, of embarrassment. Sam(a) watched Ghozala's face and wondered if she was on the verge of pouncing on Lilia. Then Sam(a) continued to wonder if it was good or bad to be fat in Egypt in the 1930s, or if Lilia was just a characteristically harsh, regimented person. In the modern day, when Sam(a) had gone to Egypt after Wassim's death, before she left in haste, there were advertisements on the TV in her hotel room that closed in on a woman's butt as she sauntered up a street. And in some parts of the world — far enough from Egypt — families force-fed their daughters to marry them off. In the United States, men often seemed to like to have sex with curvy women and marry skinny bodies, particularly with moments of manufactured fat.

'And then his sad story about the economic crisis!' she said. 'We all tightened the belt, but people will always need clothes! I don't believe they're doing poorly. And what's more, if I were a dirty old man and wanted to get my hands all over young girls, you know what I'd do? I'd open a Monsieur Edouard's and cover all the windows like that.'

'Would you prefer that we all just be naked,' Ghozala said.

' عيب ' - eib - shame on you, Lilia said, taking an emphatic bite of hawawshi.

24. Bed 01100010 01100101 01100100 00001010

'THE BEACH CLOSES AT SUNDOWN. LEAVE THE BEACH IMMEDIATELY,' a patrol officer said over a loudspeaker from his tiny buggy. I had not heard him over the crashing of the waves and the sound of Tony's performative, throaty breathing in my ears. 'THE PENALTIES FOR TRESPASSING AFTER DARK RANGE FROM FINES TO PRISON TIME. YOU WILL BE PROSECUTED TO THE FULLEST EXTENT OF THE LAW. I REPEAT: YOU WILL FACE PROSECUTION.'

'ALRIGHT, SIR!' Tony shouted, hopping to his feet. He offered me a hand up off the sand. 'What a power hungry little man!'

Satisfied by the sight of our moonlit silhouettes leaving the premises back to the lamplit boardwalk, the patrol buggy sped away. It stopped again in the far distance, the little red light atop the buggy flashing like a star. 'THE BEACH CLOSES AT SUNDOWN,' the patrol officer repeated to someone unseen — perhaps another couple that needed to get a room. *How can a beach close at night like a shop?* I wondered. The idea of nature opening and closing to the public puzzled me like the idea of private beaches and islands. *Everything in this society is a commerce. Everything under heaven these days.*

'Imagine — All of this fuss over an orgasm,' I said. 'I took a Mandarin course in college, and one of the few phrases I can remember is a four-word colloquialism— called 成语 - cheng yu — in Chinese grammar: '小事大作' - *xiaoshi dazuo*.

'What's that mean?' Tony asked.

'Much ado about nothing,' I said.

'Sex isn't nothing,' Tony said. 'You know how many patients I see whose lives have been ruined by sex?'

'Oh certainly, it's important and can be devastating — but an orgasm lasts a few seconds at most. And yet you and I are spending the entire evening jumping through hoops for a few seconds. It's not nothing, but it's certainly no reason to almost get arrested on Brighton Beach and put on some sex offender list,' I said. 'For me, it's like the first time I cooked spinach. I bought a big bushel of it, boiled it, and saw it reduce to a little dish of nothing. 小事大作.'

'Is sex just about orgasming? Your foreplay felt soulful for someone who races to the finish line?' Tony said.

'That's the kindest thing anyone has ever told me,' I said.

'It's not just your foreplay,' Tony said. 'When you were high in the restaurant earlier, I could tell you'd be a soulful lay. You're sad like a Beach House ballad. I wanted you from the jump.'

'Me too, honestly. You look so beautiful and distinguished in your little suit — like a gentleman from another era,' I said. 'I feel like I'm ruining this and at any moment you're gonna bounce.'

'I'd never do that to you,' he said.

I instantly sobered myself after he said this and became stone-faced and silent. I turned my face from him into the shadowland just out of the throw of the boardwalk's lamplight. I let the darkness kiss and caress my cheek as it always had when men like Tony fail to make good on their promises. 甜嘴巴 - tian zuiba - sweet talker (literally sweet mouth in Chinese), was another of the few Mandarin phrases I had committed to memory since college. My Chinese language professor said once that linguistic research shows that if you're exposed to a word on seven separate occasions, it enters the long-term memory. How many times then had I thought about sweet talkers?

We had passed the point on Brighton Beach where the former Soviet Union emigres stroll along the would-be Baltic of the pre-1990s. We were headed on the boardwalk toward the point where Coney Island's entertainments are — funnel cakes and frozen lemonade, the rides at Luna Park, an aquarium that was probably closed. There was nothing and no one between those two points — just a no-man's land and two gay people looking for a place to fornicate in a city with a vast, unreliable public transportation system.

'You still on your app?' Tony asked.

'Yeah, nothing,' I said. 'But I'm on it.' I pulled my phone out of my back pocket, dusted off some of the sand from our would-have-been sex on the beach and fired up Pound. Nothing.

'Have you ever had sex in public?' I asked. 'Successfully.'

'A few times,' Tony said.

'Oh yeah? Anything remarkable?' I asked.

'Yes,' Tony said. 'I was at a summer camp in the South of France. I did it in a lavender field. He was my first.'

'Sounds precious,' I said.

'It was, actually,' Tony said. 'A lot of bees though. How about you? Or was this your first attempt?'

154

'No, no,' I said.

Months had passed since I lost my virginity in the little sedan in Sunset Park. I ventured into Manhattan. There was a gay bar downtown that I had been to once before. That night, there was an underwear theme, and for some reason there were soap suds everywhere. I can't recall why there were soap suds, or who was making and releasing them into the hubbub of young, gay bodies, but I know that there was a poster for the event outside that made it sound cute and quippy. I read the poster while I smoked a cigarette in only my underwear and down coat. I was freezing. He tapped on the window just behind the poster, startling me. We had grown up in the same synagogue community. He was also Egyptian. His mother was Puerto Rican. She had converted from Catholicism to Judaism to be with his father. I felt a great sense of relief to see him there. He was like a lifesaver in a sea of sweating, soapy bodies, clumsily slithering around each other. We shared two drinks. I wanted another cigarette. We didn't have to go outside he said. Behind the bathrooms was a utility door that he opened, and inside there was a writhing pit of bacchanalia. We sat together on a crate of empty bottles. We watched. I had sex with him more than once that night, in a corner of the room, batting away the others. I texted him the next day. He wanted to have sex again, he said. I asked if he loved me. He never texted back. I saw him a few years later in Soho, jaunting through the streets with some blond guy, laughing like they were having a grand time.

'I lost my virginity to an older dude in a car not far from here,' I said. 'Not quite a lavender field, and no bees.'

'You win some, you lose some, am I right' Tony said.

I didn't answer. I wondered who between us had lost some. As for me, I had lost nothing more than my virginity.

My Pound app made a popping sound. The notification on my phone informed me that I had one new message. I opened the app.

A photo of a bed. Nothing. No caption.

Hi, I wrote.

A moment later, a photo of a headless naked body. Well worked-out.

A moment later, a *Hi,* in response.

Any face picture? I asked. *We're two guys here, looking for someone to host.*

No face pic, the profile said. *No one knows about me. I have to be very discreet.*

I'm almost certain I don't know anyone you know, bro, I said.

Sorry, bud. No can do, he replied.

Well we can't be meeting up with faceless people. I'm sure you can appreciate that. I of course appreciate your need for discretion, I said.

Nothing. Silence.

'What's going on?' Tony asked.

'A faceless dude. I told him there was no way we'd consider it without a face pic,' I said. 'He's got kind of a nice bed though.' I showed Tony the pic.

'Ha!' Tony exclaimed. 'It is a nice bed. And he has a nice body.'

'But no face — a bit creepy, right?' I said.

'Yeah, you're right — No way,' Tony said. 'But it's good to know we've got an option.'

I looked at the photo of the bed. Very neatly made, like something out of a furniture catalogue. Maybe it was the weed and liquor or all our walking and talking, but I suddenly wanted to sleep in it. Alone.

25. Closed Port - Huis Clos

It seemed to Sam(a) that her grandfather Wassim was always on his way out the door, out of Alexandria, running to catch an outbound train, headed southward, falling deeper into the country. He was chronically late for work. No time to chat. Shaking a tail feather, straightening up to fly right.

But if Wassim and Sam(a) did chat, what would Sam(a) tell him? She often wondered.

I'm your grandson. I have a vagina right now, but I'm a (gay) man. Horrible things will happen in the next decade. You'll try to rebuild a life around the globe. You'll fail, but the most workable solution will become the United States. Freewheeling, whimsical things will happen there that you won't understand or wish to recognise, in your enduring 1930s Alexandria of the mind, and you'll end up raising your grandson. Then you'll die — by no fault of your own, of course — and that grandson will live out the rest of his life like a ghost, joining his howls to the melancholy winds of Brighton Beach.

Sam(a) weighed a big reveal on occasion. In New York, depression and anxiety never seemed to exist for Wassim. One was either normal or crazy. That is to say, the Saadouns were intransigent about mental health — or rather that people ignore and hide away the depression and anxiety that challenges most humans to various degrees. Imagine what the outcome of Sam(a) revealing her situation to Wassim would be if he didn't simply have Sam(a) committed to a mental health sanatorium. The Saadouns were at once progressive enough to believe in science, aware that science cannot explain everything, and in the frustrating position of inheriting a great many para-religious folk beliefs to fill in those gaps with magical thinking. Imagine if some obscure folktale in the Saadoun family's canon of superstitions explained time travel and made Sam's presence in that time and place comprehensible to Wassim. Sam(a) on occasion, imagining this possibility, fantasised that Wassim would have shorn his grandson's hair, instructed him to bind his breasts, dressed him in a fine suit and tarboush, and taken him along on his grandiose voyages across their motherland, tied Sam to the earth beneath them with a *Diarios de Motocicleta - Motorcycle Diaries* sojourn to know intimately all the peoples that, in the sum of them, are Egyptian. As things were, if Sam(a) so much as bid good day to the flower shop boy of Flower Street, her great aunt Lilia would explode in furore and shame. It was when Sam(a) felt trapped in the house on Flower Street that she thought revealing herself to her family might free her from that situation, if it did not blow their sweet, old-fashioned minds, like the disappearance of a couple of women around their neighbourhood.

It frequently seemed to Sam(a) that they had all found greater degrees of freedom from her gilded cage on Flower Street. Wassim was especially free. For his job at the shipping company, Wassim took trains to the towns and villages across Lower Egypt — everywhere that runs from Alexandria, along the single artery of life that is the Nile, down past Cairo to cities like Helwan and Minya. There, he supplied dressmakers and costumiers like Monsieur Edouard's with catalogues of foreign-designed textiles, many of which used Egyptian-grown cotton. He took orders, and he returned to Alexandria to arrange shipments by post. Wassim's cross-country travels stood in stark contrast to the expectation that Sam(a) not leave her home. Even the other girls were better off. Ghozala worked as a nurse's assistant at a hospital. Lilia took classes to learn typing and shorthand. Ayoub escorted them to work and to school. And owing to the missing women in the news, he also escorted them home each day.

In his late 40s, Ayoub was retired from his work as an accountant. When he was not in demand for his services as a cantor, he spent his days at the synagogue, reading psalms. The night before a cantor gig — at a Shabbat, a wedding, or a bar mitzvah — Lilia or Ghozala would prepare a single glass containing a raw egg in his room for Ayoub to drink. He did this to coat his vocal cords. Lilia would leave it on his nightstand, under a lamp. The first time Sam(a) saw the glowing egg in a glass, she became entranced — drawn to the illuminated ball of sunshine, suspended in its translucent egg white. She wondered what sort of Ancient Egyptian magic it had been. Once inside the room, she recognised it as an egg yolk, but then her attentions were drawn to Ayoub's desk, which sat before a window overlooking Flower Street. On it was the mysterious package he had brought home together with the parcel of fabric that would make her deep red dress at Monsieur Edouard's. Just as her hand reached the parcel's rough, fibrous paper, Ayoub cleared his throat from the doorway. Taken aback, she left immediately. They said nothing to each other.

'You are of course quite welcome in this house, and my

grandmother has been so safe and sane since you arrived,' Lilia told Sam(a) the next day. Lilia said this in a seemly whisper, as she and Sam(a) washed and dried dishes. 'But you must understand that baba is very private about his things. You'll do well to stay out of his room. I only go there when absolutely necessary to bring him his egg tonic.' And so it was that Sam(a)'s small world became one room smaller.

In the day, Sam(a) reflexively made herself useful. The expectation that she would cook or clean was unspoken, since the Saadouns would never verbally require that a guest in their home work for room and board. Yet it seemed to Sam(a) that over time, dishes began to pile up and clothes went unwashed, and no one said a word to stop her when everything seemed to fall into place by the time the Saadouns returned home. Adam, who smoked in bed all day, would not look her in the face, even when she joined Hawa to bring him his meals. Sam(a) was left to clean the home or to wander the back yard with Hawa and discourage her, with frequency, from wandering the neighbourhood. It became apparent to Sam(a) that old as Hawa was, she never grew accustomed to living in a finite space.

Sam(a) had heard in her youth that you can keep a goldfish from growing by keeping it in a small bowl. Hawa's body was small. She had come of age in lean times, and her rib cage had not expanded much past prepubescence. Still, Hawa made known, each time she broke loose into the surrounding neighbourhood of Cleopatra, that she was too large in other senses to live and die in a bed with a chain-smoking old man, even a bed tucked behind such a stately, bourgeois home on the Alexandrian coast.

Everyday at around 10 in the morning, Sam(a) and Hawa found themselves sitting at the dining room table, drinking coffee. Sam(a) felt on occasion that she was fishing for information from Hawa, in the way that a journalist would. She had discovered, for instance, that her family was almost consistently lactose intolerant, which explained why Sam(a) never enjoyed a New York slice. Over time, as she grew more comfortable with her great great grandmother, Sam(a)'s line of questioning became more probing and frank. Sam(a) had lost the veneer of propriety, filial piety, and awe that had once served as a barrier between them.

'When you leave like you do, when you go wandering the neighbourhood, not the back yard, what happens in your mind?' Sam(a) asked. 'Is it a powerful emotion? Do you feel something click in your head? Is it a kind of claustrophobia or a loneliness?'

'It's an emotion. A very powerful feeling,' Hawa said. 'I couldn't tell you exactly which emotion exactly, although there is some exhilaration as I run through the alleyway into the street. I don't want to be caught, you see. And that's exciting. They say I'm crazy, as you know, so maybe that's it.'

'I also feel a bit claustrophobic lately. Maybe it's because I have so much time to think. Maybe it's because of the strange way I came to be here — neither here nor there. But I'm beginning to feel a bit crazy,' Sam(a) said.

'Never say that!' Hawa exclaimed, with intent, chiding eyes. 'Never tell anyone you're crazy! Even if you do have something like that inside you, you have to quiet it. It's when people start calling you crazy that you find trouble, and there's no returning from that trouble. Do you understand my meaning?'

'Not at all' Sam(a) said. 'What sort of trouble?'

'Take me for instance: The moment I became crazy for this family — That's to say, the moment people started saying it and not just thinking it — I fell backward in time... That's probably even more confusing. Let me explain: You're tired of being in this house and cooking and cleaning and seeing the same sullen faces everyday. I was like you. For an eternity. A good girl. And then one day, something glorious happened, something snapped. I had always asked myself why life is as it is, but for the first time I answered that question: I said, it doesn't need to be this way! And I left! And no one stopped me at the door! And when someone came for me and brought me back by reminding me that I supposedly need a place to sleep and food to eat, I returned for some time, and when I had my fill of their food and shelter, I left again to my wandering. And I do love to imagine, when I return to the road, that I have proven my children wrong — that I don't need their food and shelter, and that I am free of it. But then, when my constant leaving became a nuisance for the family, when they became tired of finding me, I became nuts, for them. Nuts for leaving. And then they made it harder to leave. They all started watching and commenting and setting little rules to hold me back and chasing after me before I'd been very far. My own children started to watch me like a child. At one point, I thought there was a freedom in being crazy and that running out into the street was a mad rush of joy. But I've

163

learned after so many times of breaking loose, that madness is a temporary freedom. It's a trap.'

'But you still break loose. You told me just this morning that you were thinking to break loose. You asked me to come with you!' Sam(a) said.

'A temporary freedom is better than no freedom,' Hawa said.

'I suppose,' Sam(a) said. She drank her coffee, deep in thought. 'It's not just the wandering though, right? When I first arrived, you started saying random things — you spoke of Brookli and the moon.'

'Sometimes I have like a twitch, and I feel I need to say something. That part is, as you put it, like something clicking in my head. Or maybe it comes from somewhere beyond me, and I receive it somewhere in my mind or my heart. Maybe I'm crazy, maybe they're right,' Hawa said.

'I see,' Sam(a) said. Sam(a) wanted to comfort Hawa, but she feared that telling her that she was sane would embolden her to try to escape the house again.

'Anyway, I'm just one example of what happens when they start calling you crazy. There was poor Samia,' Hawa said.

'Samia?' Sam(a) asked.

'The mother of the children,' Hawa said. 'My son's wife, Heaven rest her. A very delicate and breakable woman.'

Wassim had never spoken of his mother, except to say that she had died when he was a child. Sam(a) had always assumed that this was owing to his superstitions: They never spoke of death in their home, out of the belief that speaking of things welcomes more of the same. It was on this principle that they followed many of their sentences with Heaven-willing or Heaven-forbid, as a function of their Egyptian-American grammar.

'Samia my daughter-in-law went crazy and died, they say,' Hawa said. 'They say.'

'Crazy? How?' Sam(a) asked. She had never heard this before. Sam(a) was astounded that Wassim had kept his mother's story from her. It had been an enduring secret — one that lasted for Sam(a)'s little over three decades of life before Wassim died. Wassim so often spoke of Egypt. He spoke of Egypt like one speaks unrelentingly, with a lovesick heart, of the loss of the only thing one can have known to have been true. A lot of repetition. And he had never mentioned Samia. Sam(a) never even knew her name, which so closely resembled Sam, her birth name. But then again, Hawa, who sat before Sam(a) at the dining room table, would also become a shadow person, in Brooklyn, where they kept a photo of Adam in a place of honour. There was not a single reminder of who Hawa had been — not in a frame, not tucked away in an album with other hidden things. Nothing and nowhere at all.

'Exactly — crazy how?' Hawa said. 'It happened before they built Adam and I the flat in the back of the house: Samia became crazy and died, they said. I asked what they meant by crazy. I asked time and again. They told me only that she would become enraged with my son. Especially in the summer, they said. She became very angry with him, and then she died. I don't ask questions, but it doesn't make sense to me. Poor thing. I liked her a lot.'

'Did she have a reason to become angry?' Sam(a) asked.

'I don't ask about their personal affairs. It's unbecoming, even for a mother, to pry into a couple's marital issues. My son is a stern man, a bit of a particular personality. You must know, that despite my confusion over what happened to his wife, and despite whatever happened, he is a good man. I am certain of it. But I know that in the summer, I also become angry. There are things you don't understand, my dear — but in the summer, when it's hot, and you have to share your bed with a man, it makes you hate life, Heaven forgive me,' Hawa said. 'You feel the heat from their man body, smell their perspiration, and you want to shout and leave.'

Sam(a) nodded. She had experienced this sensation in New York, with gay men. Hawa spoke on her seasonal misandry like it was a universal feeling experienced by all partnered women, but Sam(a) suddenly felt that it was a hereditary characteristic of the Saadoun women — and other femme Saadouns.

'Does that make you crazy?' Hawa asked. Her tone indicated that this was not a rhetorical question. Sam(a) had no answer. Sam(a) also wanted to know.

Sam(a) thought about the package in Ayoub's room. Ayoub was a curious man. Quiet.

'It's not your fault, Sam(a),' Hawa said, suddenly. It was another of Hawa's curious non sequiturs.

'What do you mean?' Sam(a) asked. 'What's not my fault?'

Hawa paused for a moment.

'You know what — I don't know? I just felt I had to say it. Like Brookli over the moon!' Hawa said, mouth agape. Hawa took Sam(a)'s hand and continued speaking, 'I felt overcome by a need to tell you: It wasn't your fault, my child. You couldn't have known.'

Sam(a) and Hawa were startled by the sound of the front

door slamming shut.

'I'm home,' Wassim called out from the foyer. 'My train got in just a moment ago,' he said from entryway leading from the hall into the dining room. He wore a suit and tarboush and carried a briefcase and a large brown paper bag with a grease stain on one side.

'Let us fix you some lunch, rouhi,' Hawa said. 'You must be hungry after your travels.'

'I bought lunch on Tigran Basha,' he said.

'Alright, my son. If you prefer to eat trash than your grandmother's cooking, I'll bring you a plate so you can eat like a human. And a cup of tea,' Hawa said. Not everything in her had burst into rebellion with old age, Sam(a) thought. She had only ever known a life of servitude.

A moment of awkward silence passed. Sam(a) and Wassim exchanged polite smiles.

Sam(a) thought to take this opportunity to say something meaningful to her grandfather. It was rare that they had a chance to speak at length. Sam(a) wondered if Hawa had left them alone for so long because Hawa knew that Sam(a) craved an opportunity to have a full-fledged conversation with her young grandfather. Either that, or she had forgotten that she had promised her grandson a plate and tea. Or she had decided against her promise of domesticity and she was at that very moment crossing the large avenues to the corniche to watch the waves and passersby.

Sam(a) asked Wassim about his travels.

'Are you especially interested in travel?' Wassim asked.

'Yes, very much,' Sam(a) replied. 'It's very quiet in the house in the daytime.'

'Poor girl. You must be very bored. When I have a few days off, the whole family will go to the cinema. Or there's an amusement park just south of the city called El Negoum that is delightful.'

'That would be nice, but I do want to hear about your travel,' Sam(a) pressed. In his old age, Wassim would repeat stories of these travels time and again. Sam(a) wondered, *What is it about old people that makes some of them love to recount their travels or the plot lines of films they have seen? Is it a kind of anxiety or are they trying to assert to younger people that they're still capable of memory?* The answer was that in his youth, Wassim left himself no time for reminiscences. What he had lived a moment earlier was immaterial, particularly in Alexandria, where a great many exciting, sexy, and poetic things were constantly coming to pass. Only later, in other cities and in his 30s, would he begin to live a backward-facing life.

'Well, I believed I would be home yesterday evening,' he began. 'I took an early morning train out of the city, through Damanhour to Tanta. From there, I took several busses and cars to about nine villages around the city. But at one of the villages, they wouldn't let me in without proof of vaccination, and I left my card at home, so I had no choice but to submit to a second vaccine! The whole village and I were waiting for the vaccine in a large tent at the village's edge. I made friends with the village druggist, Mister Mohsen. We waited for our jabs for hours, and when it was done Mister Mohsen insisted that I come to dinner with his family, and I felt it would have been undignified to say no, and I was quite hungry. So that

168

night, I stayed at a hotel in Tanta, which is beautiful at night — not like Alex, but there's some night life.'

Sam(a) had heard this story about the vaccination before, several times. She remarked that the details would remain the same — accurate to their origins, even decades later.

'I'm sorry,' Wassim said. 'Do you mind if I eat while I speak? I've got to get back to work after lunch.'

'Please — I'm sorry to keep you. It's just I love stories of grand adventures like this,' Sam(a) said.

Wassim retrieved the brown paper bag and from inside it, he produced a sandwich wrapped in more paper still.

'What are you eating?' Sam(a) asked.

'A falafel and ful sandwich from Bishara's on Tigran Basha,' Wassim said. 'My sisters will tell you I am the king of falafel. It's my favourite thing.'

Sam(a) suddenly had the sensation of falling. It was as though her reality — the time travel or the world created in her mind or whatever hypnosis was — was dissolving before her. And yet Wassim and Alexandria were still there when she closed and reopened her eyes. They were still clutching her by the oesophagus. Sam(a) could not let Wassim see her cry. She would allow herself what femininity her situation had imposed on her, but to have been brought before her grandfather only to cry would have been too cruel a punishment, she thought.

'I am sorry to cut our talk short, but I should run and see what's happened to your grandmother,' Sam(a) said, breathless. Wassim stood as Sam(a) exited the room, in a show of his European education and politesse, but he was not upset to cut things short. Quite the contrary, he was happy to eat his sandwich in peace and return to work.

In the back yard, Sam(a) searched not for her great-great-grandmother, who had by then wandered from the corniche back inland to Luxor Street, and had begun telling strangers her life story. They offered her coffee, she told them what they took to be their fortunes, spun of her own experiences mixed with theirs.

Sam(a) found the bush from whence she had sprung on her first night in this place. She wiped the tears from her face. She held her breath. Steadying herself, she pushed her arms into the thick brush before her and felt her skin punctured and torn amid by thorns and nettles. She pulled the foliage aside resolutely set on returning herself to New York in the 21st century. She plunged herself into the brush deeply and without concern for her pain, and there behind the bushes, she found only the wall of the adjacent building and the dirt from whence the bush sprang. She felt panic set in her chest. She had paid Doctor Fahmy a pretty penny and convinced her to amend her usual practice to make a choice that would become a prison.

26. The Air الهوا

Hawa first barrelled down the alley beside the Saadoun home. Her steps were adroit and silent. She had learned from experience that the more one hesitates, the greater the risk of making a scene. So like a mighty wind and with purpose, she made for the sea. She ran across one large avenue. A car several yards away honked its horn at her, but it was moving much more slowly than the winged Hawa, small, wrinkled, and agile, wrapped in her black cloak, face like a warrior. She made a gesture as if to flick the automobile aside with her hand. She had existed before the automobile. She was the Queen of Cleopatra. 'Village idiot,' she muttered under her breath, as she looked back to catch a glimpse of the impudence that would dare honk at her. It was a young dandy. She felt she could easily defeat him with her fists alone, if she encountered him on his two feet.

Hawa caught her breath at the small island in the middle of the grand thoroughfare that ran past the corniche, and then she ran again to the Mediterranean. She looked at the marvellous infinity of the sea, felt the wind on her face and listened to the sound of the waves crashing against rocks. Then she grew bored of that, and she reckoned that the Saadouns or the Sam(a) girl would realise she was gone and that the corniche would be the first place they would look to find her. Again, she was off, her black cloak floating in the wind, like a superhero cape.

Hawa could not return via Flower Street. She had to take a detour. One block up, she saw the Eliyahou Hazan Synagogue, she kissed her hand and raised it to the building, for good measure. Finally, she hit a large street called Luxor, made a right and then a left on El Delta. Then she found herself on Tigran Basha, where everyone knew her.

'Here she comes — the Witch of Flower Street,' Mahmoud the sugar cane juice vendor told Charbel the فطاير - fatayer - savoury pie vendor at the stall next door. 'Go tell her your problems. Just be warned, she doesn't have all day.'

Charbel had been waiting for Hawa. He had two 20 piastre coins ready, a spinach pie in a small brown bag, and a كنكه - kanaka - coffee pot brewing on the stove in the back of his shop. It was just before the lunch rush, so Charbel and Mahmoud sat, as they did every day, on the steps outside their shops, chain-smoking and complaining. Both Charbel and Mahmoud thought that the other was a complainer and fancied himself to be an easygoing man, matching the other's sour mood. But they were getting each other down and had no choice but to continue to complain their days away. Their relationship was premised — like their livelihoods — on bellyaching.

'Oh Ms. Hawa!' Mahmoud called out, beckoning to her. 'My friend Charbel would like to speak with you. He needs your special sight.'

'I don't know how much time I have to speak to Charbel, my sons,' Hawa said, looking up Tigran Basha to Flower Street to see if she was being followed by Sam(a) or Wassim. 'Make it quick.'

'What is it that makes you run this way? Is it the spirits

that chase you?' Mahmoud asked, on the verge of laughter. He only half-believed in her fortunetelling, mostly because it never resembled fortunetelling, and yet it was always worth the two 20 piastre coins, because it helped to pass the time when business was slow.

'Never you mind why I run! My private business is my business and yours is yours,' she said. 'I don't ask your business unless you want answers, isn't that so?'

'I would like to ask you about a matter of the heart,' Charbel said, directing her into his shop and offering her a seat. Mahmoud stood at the entrance to Charbel's shop, an eager audience, already smiling, thinking on her previous fortunes, none of which had informed his future, all of which had been thoroughly hilarious to him. On a small table in front of her, Charbel placed the small paper bag with a spinach pie and two small porcelain cups on saucers.

'Thank you, my son,' she said.

'Thank you, Ms. Hawa,' he replied, placing the 20 piastre pieces in her hand. Hawa put them into a pocket hidden beneath her cloak. Charbel sat and observed her. She took two bites of the spinach piece and downed the Turkish coffee.

'*A woman who is unafraid of heat is afraid of no man!* So it was said, in the old times,' she remarked. Charbel followed suit, downing his coffee in one go. He scalded his tongue. His pain emerged only as a watering of the eyes. Hawa observed Charbel and made mental notes. Charbel removed his coffee cup and saucer from the small table and offered them to Hawa.

'What would you have me do with these?' she said, straight-faced. 'I have done my share of dishes, son.'

'You use them to read the future?' Charbel asked.

'I don't need to play children's games to see the truth,' Hawa said. 'Tell me your troubles.'

'There is a girl from my church. Céline. We have been chatting before services on Sunday for weeks. Finally, I asked her if she would like for us to be married. She says that I don't have enough money to raise a family, selling spinach pies. What do I do?' he asked.

'I see,' Hawa said. 'Well listen and listen good, Charbel: Very long ago, I was a young girl, do you understand?'

Charbel nodded. He looked with great seriousness into Hawa's face. Mahmoud put one hand into his pocket and pinched his outer thigh with just enough pressure to stop himself from laughing.

'I was walking outside of Alexandria — in the countryside, you know,' she continued. 'And a man, young but several years my senior called to me from across a small stream coming from the Nile. He said, "Hey, you girl, how do I get to the other side?"' Hawa performed the young man's voice as a rumbling thunder, deep from within her chest. It startled Charbel to hear it.

'Do you want to know how I answered?' Hawa asked. A moment passed. Charbel was uncertain that she wanted him to answer.

'He does,' Mahmoud said.

'I said, "You are on the other side, idiot!"'

Charbel looked down at the table, trying to make sense of things. Mahmoud inspected his fingers to see if he had drawn blood, pinching himself, but the moisture was only the sweat of his palms.

'What does it mean, Ms. Hawa?' Charbel asked.

'Come on, dear boy,' Hawa said. 'You know very well what it means — What it means is for you to know, better than I will know and your friend Mahmoud will know and your friend Salwa can ever know, and that's the idea, you know?'

Deep in thought, Charbel nodded and looked to the ground, still searching for answers.

'I have to go now, my sons,' Hawa said, putting the remainder of her spinach pie in the bag and tucking it away in a pocket of the frock she wore beneath her cloak. Mahmoud helped her to her feet. Hawa put her hand, like a tangle of bronze wires, on Charbel's shoulder, leaned into his ear and said, 'You are on the other side, sweetheart.'

And with that, Hawa vanished like the Phantom of Flower Street, down Tigran Basha, in the direction of Sidi Gaber station.

As late as the 1970s, Mahmoud, who suffered from macular degeneration, would tell his grandchildren that he thought he saw Ms. Hawa, the whimsical woman from the before-times, scurrying along Tigran Basha. But then he would find that it had been an optical illusion or the sea wind in his eyes.

27. Breakthrough - Durchbruch

You can't choose when you get off a ferris wheel, unless of course you jump. Most of the time, you're stuck there, wishing life — or at least time— away. And it is of course a sin to wish Heaven's gifts away. But then, so many things are sins, in the Arab faiths — faiths with a dizzying number of rules — exported internationally. Or maybe the fault does not lie with faith. Maybe sin came naturally to me. Or maybe multiple realities coexisted contemporaneously, like the physicists' and Doctor Fahmy's idea of the multiverse.

As we passed the dark limbo between Brighton Beach and Coney Island, I felt the energy had shifted. Maybe it was the flashing lights emanating from Luna Park's rides. I felt very strongly that the entire universe seemed happier on that side of the boardwalk. From somewhere in the periphery of our visions — Tony's and my own — two young men in wheelchairs raced in the direction of the Coney Island Parachute Jump. The sounds of their wheels rolling across the boardwalk planks was percussive. Tony looped his arm around me and held me by the waist. I could feel the coldness of his hands inspecting the parts of me where fat had accumulated. I put my hand on his, tore it from my flesh and held it.

'Your hands are so cold — Are you cold?' I asked, pretending to be a sweeter, softer sort of person.

'I'm good,' he said. His tone suggested that he was aware of my little caprices.

I rubbed his hand between mine in a half-hearted show of consideration, and then I relinquished it, gave him back what was his and returned to myself what was mine. Luna Park was still crowded, and all of the vendors still open.

'Shall we?' Tony asked.

'You want to go on the rides?' I asked.

'Of course, I do — I have a soul,' he said.

Somewhere deep inside, I also wanted to go on the rides. It had been an eternity since I had been on a ride. A grown man alone at an amusement park intended primarily for children is cause for concern, and my trips to Brighton Beach were customarily a solo endeavour.

'I want to go on the ferris wheel,' I said, and then I wondered why I had said it. And meant it. I had never been especially fond of heights. I suppose I wanted Tony to know that I was capable of childish flights of fancy. I wanted to prove to myself that I was capable of joy.

At the entrance to the park were a series of food vendors selling funnel cakes, pizza, frozen lemonades. I had never noticed before, on my usual trek to Brighton Beach, the falafel vendor. He had an Egyptian look. Egyptians look like a great many things, phenotypically speaking. What I mean to say is that he looked like a Wassim sort of man. I felt as though he would look up at Tony and I, ignore Tony and the implications of me being with him, tell me that nothing good happens late at night, and say that I better go home before I end up in the gutter. I felt a rumbling inside me, like an express train through the chest. At times, I have found myself with no choice but to get on that train into myself. At that moment, I was able to stand at the platform on what felt like solid ground and let it pass. I passed the falafel stand. It passed me.

I bought us a Luna Card. I figured that the park would soon close. I put $25 on the card, enough for a floating gondola for two on the ferris wheel and maybe some lesser rides.

'We're not going to have sex on a ferris wheel, right?' Tony said, as we emerged into the night sky. Our view of the Atlantic Ocean was so clear that I could have seen home from where we sat, gently rocking back and forth, my palms sweating a bit.

'No,' I said. 'But I got you alone.'

'At least!' Tony said. 'And no audience.'

'And no bees!' I said.

'We are blessed,' he said. I nodded and looked away.

'Is that one of your hypnosis things?' Tony asked. 'How you look away? You look into the distance like you see something there — maybe ghosts.'

'Why are you interested in me at all? In my little manners?' I asked.

'Does it upset you?' Tony asked.

I didn't know. I liked to be seen. It's rare to be seen. You can meet men on Pound and have the sensation of being invisible to them, even after you've met a few times. And yet, I felt as though I couldn't breathe that evening without Tony's analysis. It felt oppressive to me, especially knowing that he was part of an industry that gently unravels people in order to be paid to put them back together again, without the mental defects and painful memories that make us human.

'Not at all!,' I said. 'I just want to know what you get out of this? Or do you pathologise all your lays?'

Tony looked at me, speechless for a moment with searching eyes. 'I don't pathologise my lays, Sam,' he said. 'And you're not my lay. You're a man who's planning on psychologically castrating himself tomorrow. And whatever this is between you and I, you don't deserve that.'

I looked out at the ocean's majestic infinity. I thought about Wassim. I thought about how the Saadouns had been and how how Tony was. I felt a certain delicious bitterness — a superiority.

'I'm not American enough to believe I'm owed anything,' I said.

'I didn't say that you are owed anything. There's a clear distinction between entitlement and acknowledging your humanity — that you deserve to live a full life, with romance and sex and youth. You deserve happiness,' he said.

'That's not true, Tony. Happiness — life as the pursuit of happiness — is a hollow slogan of the so-called West and its shrinks. A false promise. Happiness is for weightless people. The rest of us are born to at best survive being irrevocably fucked. I'm done feeling like a mental defective for not being born blessed and full of hot air.'

The ocean winds boxed my ears, as a moment passed. Tony continued to stare at me, unflinchingly. This irritated me, immediately after my outburst. Then I felt contrite. Contrition was the way of the Saadouns. Contrition and other hard feelings.

'Want some cake?' I asked. I held out our bag of home-church kulich cakes as a peace offering. Tony took them, placed the bag in his lap, retrieved one of the two cakes, unwrapped one gingerly, broke it in half, opened his mouth wide, and popped the entire half into his mouth, cheeks puffed out like a chipmunk. I laughed, despite myself.

'Listen, Sam,' Tony said. 'I'm not speaking to you in a professional capacity. I'm speaking to you as someone who cares. This isn't therapy.'

'Then take your pants off,' I said. 'Pants are for therapists. Let's join the mile- or whatever this is-high club.'

'You're going to let me make a few observations without interruption. I'm going to speak as a friend. You aren't going to get mad. You are not crazy, Sam. And I am not always a therapist.'

I felt tired. I said nothing.

'You want to go back to Egypt, because there's nothing left for you here — because your family is all gone, right?' Tony said. 'Because there's no home left for you?'

I nodded.

'What was Egypt, for your family?' Tony asked.

I stared at him.

'When did your family leave Egypt?' Tony asked.

'In the 1950s,' I said. 'Never.'

'I'm no expert, but I'd imagine a few things to be true: Egypt was very different in the 1950s,' he said. 'Has it ever occurred to you that you'd arrive, discover that nothing is the same, and fall into a deep feeling of crisis there?'

'I've already had that experience and survived it. I'd rather die there than here. I'd rather have my body join the soil of my ancestors than continue to crowd the soil of others,' I said.

'There's an important logical fallacy in your thinking,

180

Sam,' Tony said. 'The idea of return. If you are trying to return to what your family was, does it make sense to render yourself asexual first? They were sexual people, Sam. Your ancestors had sex. Or you wouldn't be here.'

'What point are you trying to make, Tony?' I asked.

'My point is that it strikes me that your hypnosis tomorrow isn't what you actually want. It's some sort of self-flagellation, maybe — maybe latent homophobia. But you want to go back to an abstract place —not even just a place, a time — when your family — when your lot and you — existed. And your family was young back then. And happy. And it may be hard to hear, but logically speaking, they were also probably sexual. Making yourself something unnatural isn't going to bring you closer to them. Quite the opposite,' he said.

The wind rocked our little air gondola. I looked out to the ocean. I could see Alexandria. I had never seen Alexandria.

Tony handed me the other half of the kulich he had devoured. Our fingers grazed each other.

'Your hands are so cold,' he said. He got up and the whole cabin began to quake. I envisioned us falling off the ride to our deaths. I felt the sensation of falling in the base of my pants, in my chest, in my forearms.

'Please no!' I shouted.

I saw death. I raged against it. I had not realised I was thoroughly afraid of heights until that moment. Still, he squeezed next to me, his arm wrapping around my back and holding me tightly to generate warmth between us. I enjoyed the feeling of the kulich cake in my hand as I ate it. It was sort of like a brioche — a warm, eggy, lightly sweet flavour. A little stale.

'Sam, you like Brighton Beach not because of Russia or the Soviet Union or Socialist Realist souvenirs or unusual cakes. Those are all minor details,' Tony said.

'What is it then?' I asked.

'You've said several times tonight you've been told by some person or website or whatever that Brighton Beach looks like a composite of the Soviet Union or St. Petersburg before the 1990s,' Tony said.

'And?' I asked, feeling like our little cabin was in free fall.

'You're like an interstellar voyeur, Sam. You're a cosmic hawk feasting on the emotions of others and what of your sorrow you see reflected in them,' he replied. 'You like to watch people trying to get back to another time and place.'

28. Farewell وداعا

This is how they said goodbye. They had only a few minutes before he had to go.

Doctor Murad, the surgeon, and Doctor Papazian, the anaesthesiologist, allowed Sam into the pre-op room long enough for Wassim and Sam to speak. They had given Wassim drugs for the pain of his disintegrating insides, so he was less than lucid when he spoke. After a half-day of waiting, Wassim's heart rate had regulated enough for them to operate. Gallbladder surgery. Sam didn't know what a gallbladder was. He could have Googled it, but he knew better than to get bogged down in the science. Understanding what is happening does nothing to help in those moments. Sam was used to hospitals and bypass surgeries and holding his breath for the duration of surgeries, sitting in the cafeteria pushing around pallid macaroni salad with a fork. From Sam's early youth, it had been this way. To say he had become used to it would be inaccurate and laughable. But over the decades, Sam had familiarised himself with the hospital cafeteria and its little salad bar. A certain cynicism had grown over him like scar tissue, but he was always just as broken, during every surgery.

In the days before this final goodbye, it was November. The air was crisp and the sky a glassy blue. Sam was in his late 20s. For years, he had begun to feel the weight of caring for

Wassim bear down on him, much as Wassim tried to manage his limited mobility and entreat Wassim to go out and live as Wassim had — an eventful and adventurous sort of life. Sam had fallen into a protracted dejection about his life — a submission to how things had ended up for him and for Wassim. But in November, after the suffocating summer heat had subsided, he felt recklessly optimistic about life. Wassim would die someday, he thought — everyone would. They were the last of their family, and Sam would never have his own children. He had cared for enough people for one lifetime. Under the crystal skies of November, Sam resolved to live what of life was left to the Saadouns to the fullest. So Sam thought to make Wassim the homemade falafel that Wassim frequently said he craved when he was eating sensible steamed chicken and rice. What is the point of living a lot of a little life? Sam thought.

One November day, Sam came home with a bag of fresh fava beans from Balady supermarket in Bay Ridge. Wassim had forgotten how to make falafel from scratch. By the time Sam was born, Wassim and his wife had already developed cholesterol and a parade of other health problems that made falafel a rare decadence. On occasion, they bought dietetic boxed falafel mix from the supermarket and upon trying the finished product would proclaim that it was nothing like the real thing. Sam perused a series of Egyptian falafel recipes on his phone. Finally he arrived at a young woman on YouTube called Naima who showed only her hands as she prepared a series of Egyptian dishes — molokheya, bamia, béchamel. Before each of the major steps in her cooking, she would invoke the help of Heaven, in the same way that Wassim had taught Sam to do — an act of faith, anxiety, and magical thinking. Sam liked her voice. It was at once humorous, fed-up, and exasperated. He felt a kinship with Naima — like they could have been close friends, if the world — especially men — would have let them.

'They aren't dark enough, rouhi,' Wassim said of the finished product. 'They taste closer to the real thing than anything I've had in years! But you have to put more oil in the pan, I think. They need to be drowned in oil,' he said.

'I thought it would be better for your health to put less oil,' Sam said.

'Falafel is never going to be a health food, rouhi,' Wassim said. 'It's O.K.— You'll put more oil next time.'

In the days that followed, Wassim complained of abdominal pain. Finally, they called the ambulance. It was the gallbladder, whatever that was — some citizen of the universe of dark matter that lets us live until it decides we've run out of time.

In the pre-op room, Sam put his head on the pillow next to Wassim's and told him some things that were for them alone. Wassim did not respond. He looked into Sam's eyes with an expression of fear. In the months immediately after Wassim's death, Sam wondered if in that moment, Wassim's expression had meant he was afraid to die or if at the very end, the dying can see the future of those who will remain. Sam imagined that Wassim saw what Sam would become after Wassim died.

'Rouhi,' Wassim said. That was the only and last word he spoke in the pre-op room.

After the surgery, Doctor Murad spoke to Sam in the waiting room. Wassim had survived. But there could be no more fried foods. Ever. Sam agreed emphatically. When Doctor Murad left, Sam retreated to a corner of the waiting room to pray a psalm of thanks. Psalm 150. Somewhere in his mind, he wondered what Wassim would be like after the surgery — if that Wassim would still be Wassim. Sam wondered what his own life would be like, caring for him.

Moments later, Doctor Papazian came to the room and explained that Wassim was not breathing on his own. For hours, into the early morning, Sam waited for doctors to finally decide Wassim would not survive and to put him on morphine. Wassim was already beyond consciousness. The night nurse told Sam to go home and that she would call him if there was anything to say. On his way out of the hospital, holding Wassim's clothes and glasses in a plastic bag to his chest, he received the call.

'He's gone,' the night nurse said. The rows of stadium lights in the parking lot outside the hospital popped one-by-one in Sam's imagination, until his universe became dark.

On the road back to their apartment, the taxi driver kept looking at Sam in the rearview mirror. Sam's looked a bit shocked, like he had seen a ghost. The driver looked as though he was on the verge of saying something. Coming from the hospital late at night with a bag of belongings, the circumstances were obvious. Sam was thankful that the driver said nothing.

That night, Sam had to sleep with the lights on. In the darkness, he felt a sensation like total submersion — like drowning, like his skin was bubbling and burning. And then, for years, there was nothing at all. No sensation — pain or pleasure — to prove to Sam that he was alive or had ever lived.

Wassim would have told Sam that he was not to blame, since for Wassim, Sam was never to blame.

'Fuck them,' Wassim would say, when Sam tried to explain to his grandfather that he had been in a fight with one of his school friends and accepted responsibility for what he had done. Sam could not have been at fault, Wassim felt — although in their own arguments, Sam was always wrong. Sam never believed Wassim when he sided with Sam unflinchingly in this way. Sam understood that an immeasurable love had blinded Wassim to Sam's faults. Sam realised that if Sam did not feel contrite on his own, no one would teach him right from wrong, so he allowed himself to feel reflexively culpable for everything so as not to become an insufferable person, spoiled by love. He had inherited this innate sense of contrition from some unseen person in his history, from someone in Alexandria.

In the months that followed, Sam knew himself well enough to understand that even if he spoke to a professional who would tell him he had not killed Wassim with falafel, Sam would know for certain it was false. Anything anyone — professional or unpaid — would tell him, Sam would recognise as irrelevant and untrue words born of sympathy. He would not abide that sort of American platitude — saccharine reassurances, hollow like empty calories. So he told no one. He wanted to have killed Wassim with falafel. Late at night, sleepless in their apartment, it was easier for

Sam to understand how a night monster should feel as he did than a good man, born to live as a ghost haunting his own life.

29. Men الرجال

The knowledge that Sam(a) could not click her heels three times and return to Brooklyn sent her into a panic. She fell into the brush, thorns and nettles tearing the fine, silken fabric of her dress — one of two of Lilia and Ghozala's hand-me-downs that she owned. She slammed her hands against the soil. It failed to accept her. Alexandria of the 1930s had become a trap, she thought.

When Sam(a) came to her senses moments later, her thoughts turned to Hawa. Hawa was gone. Sam(a) thought on the missing women in the papers. She leapt to her feet, ran to the apartment at the garden's centre and knocked gently on the unvarnished wooden door. There was no answer, so she gingerly opened the door, and a cloud of smoke poured out. There, in a single room, the size of her cramped studio back in New York, Adam sat in bed, puffing at a small hand-rolled cigarette. He looked at Sam(a) with a blank stare. Sam(a) excused herself and shut the door. She ran back into the house and called for Wassim. He had finished his sandwich and left for work.

Sam(a) paced back and forth around the foyer. She had already upset Ayoub by going into his room and poking around his things. She worried that leaving without a chaperon during the day would further provoke his ire, but then so too would his mother going missing. Sam(a) thought on the large avenues between Flower Street and the corniche. There was not the sort of traffic she had seen in Cairo decades later, but Sam(a) imagined it was not impossible that a car would hit her great great grandmother as she ran for the sea. Sam(a) decided to go after her. But passing a mirror beside the front door, she noticed that her dress was torn from stomach to chest by the bush in the garden — the cosmic dead-end. Her breasts were exposed. Sam(a) ran to the bathroom that she shared with Lilia and Ghozala, removed her only remaining dress from a clothing line and changed. The residual dampness from the dress, which she had washed in the sink the night before, irritated her skin. She threw it on and ran. Passing through the front door felt like removing a corset or foot bindings. It felt like Sam(a)'s first sex in the car at the waterfront in Sunset Park. Awful and exhilarating in the certainty of consequences.

She had seldom seen the end of Flower Street. As she passed, she noted the building that would become the Chili's in Akram's Instagram messages. It had once been a sort of whimsical art deco building with rounded balconies with a middle-aged woman standing before a clothesline of laundry, supporting her sullen face on a hand on an arm perched on the balcony railing. One day, people would come to this space for Texas Cheese Fries and Diet Cokes, Sam(a) thought.

From the end of Flower Street, she could see among the bustle on the corniche that her great-great-grandmother was not there, but she figured that Hawa could have climbed over the cement barrier to the sea to sit atop the rocks on the other side. Sam(a) ran across the first large avenue and then the second. She flung herself onto the sidewalk, breathless, and scoped the rocks just over the partition. Two young boys squatted beside the sea and used bits of driftwood to prod at the creatures living between the rocks. There was no sign of Hawa, as far as the eye could see, in either direction.

'Sama!' a man exclaimed, startling her. She turned around. It was Antoun Daoudi, son of Haroun and Rachelle, wearing a fine suit under an overcoat.

'I'm Antoun — From the synagogue,' he said.

'Yes, I remember,' Sam(a) said, forcing a smile.

'You look lovely in the daylight. Are you out for a stroll?' Antoun asked.

'I was, but I have to be back. I have household duties to attend to,' Sam(a) said.

'I see,' Antoun said.

'But I'll see you on Shabbat evening?' Sam(a) said. Her Tiresian endeavour to have straight sex as a woman had been less pressing now that she had no idea how to return to what she still considered to be the present, decades into the future and a sea and an ocean away. She realised that perhaps the portal was no longer in the Saadoun garden but rather that the present could come at any moment — that Sam in the chaise in Bay Ridge could suddenly awaken from his hypnotic state and the Alexandria sky and sea and Antoun would simply vanish before she consummated her endeavour.

'I'd rather speak to you away from the synagogue,' he said. Sam(a) had already begun to cross the street to return to her search for Hawa.

'Meet me here on the corniche tonight — 10 o'clock!,' he shouted. Sam(a) shot him a thumbs up and then wondered if that meant anything in 1930s Alexandria. 'And be careful out here. The papers say women are going missing!' he shouted. Sam(a) did not turn to acknowledge this. She had already had an earful about the missing women.

Sam(a) thought on Hawa, who was more certainly missing than the disappeared ladies described in news copy from a time when the world press was given to sensationalism. Sam(a) shot out in front of a horse-drawn cart full of yams that nearly ensnared her in its wheels. Its driver lifted a hand at her and shouted, but she was already back on Flower Street, halfway to Tigran Basha before it occurred to her to shout back to the driver to say that pedestrians always have the right of way and that he knew where he could put his yams.

Approaching Tigran Basha with purpose in her step, the young man of the Flower Street flower shop appeared on the street and smiled at Sam(a) broadly like a clown. Sam(a) smiled and nodded as she passed. The young man reached out and grabbed her forearm. She turned and slapped him in the face. A reflex. Her blow was swift and firm.

'Check yourself, son,' she said in English.

Shocked, the flower shop boy released her arm. She continued on her way. Looking back from Tigran Basha, she saw him looking contrite. He waved at her sheepishly. She offered him her back. She owed him nothing. And then she imagined that he was perhaps someone's grandfather in Egypt or wherever he ended up. Still, she felt that she owed him nothing. She continued onward, past Mister Ramzi's shawarma shop, unmanned as before, radio blasting. She passed a cake shop, a Syrian ice cream stand, Mahmoud's unmanned sugar cane juice stall, and Charbel's fatayer spot. Mahmoud stood with his back to the passersby on the street at the entrance of Charbel's shop, blocking Charbel and Hawa from Sam(a)'s view. As Sam(a) passed, Hawa was eating her spinach pie and drinking the Turkish coffee that Charbel had prepared for their fortunetelling.

Sam(a) thought on the trams that come and go on Sidi Gaber. In the worst of her anxiety-fuelled fears, Sam(a) saw her grandmother standing on the tracks, distracted by the random, prescient words that seemed to suddenly pop into her head. She ran for Sidi Gaber. An unseen man at the corner of Tigran Basha whistled to her as she passed, her dress clinging to her body, which jiggled in ways to which she had not yet grown accustomed. She felt ashamed. jiggling had been shameful to her in her man body. Before, in Brooklyn, it upset her when gay men would touch her male body's waist as if to remark that there was more of it there than need be. In Alexandria, she felt that even if her female body had aroused someone, there were parts of her not tight enough to be taken seriously.

Finally, she arrived on Sidi Gaber. She wandered through crowds of people descending from a tram. Most of the passersby were men. Sam(a) was exhausted. She leaned against a wall. To her left and a few yards up the road was Monsieur Edouard's. A woman left the shop with a beautiful package wrapped in forest green monogramed paper. Hani the shop assistant bid the woman farewell. Recalling she only had one dress left, she ran up to him.

'Mister Hani, hello,' she said.

'How can I help you?' Hani asked.

'You fit me for a dress the other day. I am staying with some
relations on Flower Street,' she said.

'Ah, yes. You're the deep red dress. You're staying with the
Saadoun girls?' he asked.

'Yes, and I was wondering how much longer the dress will
take, please? Because I need it rather urgently,' she said.
Hani , who was very short, looked up into Sam(a)'s face and
thought her panic — more about Hawa than anything else
— to be about the dress.

'Let me see what I can do,' Hani said, disappearing behind
the door.

Sam(a) wanted to leave immediately and continue her
search for Hawa. But she smelled her armpits. She desperately
needed another dress. Hani reappeared and entreated her to
enter. He escorted her to the pedestal at the centre of the
room. A moment later, Ilyas appeared from behind some
black curtains. Hani disappeared to the back room.

'Mademoiselle, your dress is not ready. I need to retake some
measurements. I lost my notebook,' he said. Sam(a) nodded.
He began to wrap his tape measure around her waist.

'I need the dress as soon as possible,' she said.

Sam(a) remarked that Ilyas had a strangely attractive face
— a tall, proud nose. With the back of his hand, he seemed
to gently caress the small of her back in a way that stirred
feelings in parts of her that for all her days in Alexandria had
remained inactive.

'I can finish it for you this afternoon at no extra rush charge.
Would you like to stop by this evening?' Ilyas asked.

Sam(a) recalled her late-night rendezvous with Antoun
from the synagogue. She thought she could sneak out, lose

her lady virginity somewhere around the beach, then come get her new dress.

'How late are you open?' Sam(a) asked.

'We close in the evening before dinner. Sometimes we go later, depending on demand,' he said, measuring her thighs. Sam(a) noticed that Ilyas was not taking down her measurements. She was turned on by what she interpreted as his perversion. It had been different with Ilyas than the aggressive flower shop boy. There was a subtle horniness to Ilyas that Sam(a) appreciated.

'I live above the shop,' Ilyas said. 'You can come by when you like.'

Hani finally appeared and offered Sam(a) a bonbon. She took one and popped it in her mouth. It was a chocolate-coated marzipan nugget with a pecan at the centre. Hani lifted the dish to her again to offer her another. With her mouth still full, she lifted her hand in thanks and refused. Hani retreated with the dish.

Ilyas called out a series of numbers to Hani. Sam(a) felt upset that he had indeed been measuring her and not just taking an opportunity for his fingers to graze her curves.

'You have quite a memory, Mister Ilyas,' Sam(a) said, a bit miffed. She wondered if Ilyas was gay. She wondered if he and Hani lived together above the shop. She remarked how thrilling it would be to know what a couple of old-timey Egyptian confirmed bachelors were like.

'Our Mister Ilyas is very good with numbers and calculations,' Hani said, patting him on the back and smiling at Sam(a).

'Bravo,' Sam(a) said. 'I've never had a brain for numbers.'

Sam(a) thought on Hawa. 'I really must go,' she said. 'But I will be back for my dress late in the evening.'

A moment later, back at the street corner, beholding the passengers embarking on the tram was Hawa, Phantom of Flower Street, contemplating whether to use one of her 20 piastre pieces to jump on a tram and finally leave not just the house on Flower Street, but the neighbourhood around it and possibly the city — to see all of Egypt, Africa, and the world if she wanted, with what was left of her life, whatever the costs of such an undertaking would be. She thought with a crystal lucidity that stood in stark contrast to her family's impression of her mental faculties. When Hawa discovered Sam(a) watching her, Hawa turned to flee but hesitated. Sam(a) ran after Hawa and caught her, placing a gentle, but firm hand on Hawa's back.

Hawa's eyes searched Sam(a)'s face. Sam(a)'s did the same. There was a nonverbal exchange between them. For a moment, Sam(a) understood that the right thing to do would be to allow Hawa to flee, but then she felt she could not, for the family and for Hawa's sakes. Hawa looked at Sam(a) with a hard expression. Tears formed in her eyes, but never enough to shed onto her cheeks. Hawa would not allow it. She promised herself that one day she would leave, and that she would die as she had suddenly realised she was meant to live — without hesitation. Throngs of tramway passengers passed around them as they were locked in their small bubble. Finally, Hawa punctured that bubble when she took Sam(a)'s hand with force and squeezed it. They turned and slowly made their way back to Tigran Basha, holding hands.

Mahmoud and Charbel nodded at Hawa as she passed. She didn't nod back. She was the teacher. She owed the young men no courtesy. Sam(a) found this exchange to be curious, but she said nothing.

Farther up the street, waddling out of Ramzi's shawarma place was the short, rotund Hani.

'Mister Hani! You're everywhere, aren't you?' Sam(a) said, greeting him. He must have passed Sam(a) and Hawa unseen, cloaked in the throngs of tram passengers rushing to and from Sidi Gaber.

'Lunch!' Hani exclaimed. 'See you later, Ms. Sama!' Sam(a) nodded. Sam(a) noticed that Hani was not carrying a sandwich. She wondered how he had eaten so fast. Hawa found it strange that Sam(a) would see Hani later, but she refrained from asking questions.

As they passed the flower shop of Flower Street, the young man there saw Sam(a) and turned into the shop to sweep the floor.

Hawa released Sam(a)'s hand and passed under the marble archway beside the Saadoun home, through the alley to the back yard. Sam(a) stood for a moment to be sure that Hawa was not simply waiting for Sam(a) to retreat to the home to make a break for the wild unknown once more. When Sam(a) felt confident that Hawa had enough adventure for one day, she opened the front door and went directly to the kitchen to pour herself a glass of water.

Sitting at the kitchen table, waiting for her in silence, was Ayoub.

'Have a seat, Sama,' he said. Ayoub was not drinking or eating anything. His body was rigid and his face

expressionless. Sam(a)'s heart arose to her throat as she sank
into the chair opposite him.

30. Stillwell

'This is goodbye then,' I told Tony. We strolled along Stillwell Avenue in the direction of the Coney Island Metro station. Stillwell Avenue runs along the perimeter of Luna Park, but something about Stillwell stifles that merriment beside it. Maybe it's the ocean wind or the humid air, pregnant with water, that quiets the sonorous bells and whistles of the rides and the cacophony of children screaming to express from their chests the joy and terror of careening downward from great heights.

'I guess so,' Tony said. 'Sam, I want you to know something—'

Across the street was Nathan's Famous, where Wassim would take me for a hot dog on the first day of every summer break. We stopped walking and turned to each other. Tony took my hand and put it on his chest.

'I've dated a lot of guys, and I don't feel myself to have known any of them like I've known you in just a few hours,' Tony said.

You don't know me for shit, I thought silently. *And what you think you know, you'd soon lose patience for. And all the sweet things you tell me will return to torture me, in your absence. You'll have moved on without a second thought, because you're so calm and collected that you've made your living on it.*

'I feel the same about you,' I said. 'It's a pity.'

'That we met too late,' Tony said.

I nodded. 'And that I'm not a dumb kid anymore,' I said. 'And that everything ends.'

'I'll never stop being a hopeless romantic,' Tony said.

'Then you must be a glutton for punishment,' I said.

Tony said nothing.

I imagined what it would be like to let this one go. I hoped that our subways were on different platforms or that my train would leave first. I wanted to be the one to leave him. I resolved myself to get on whatever train in whatever direction, as long as it left before Tony's. From there, I would wait at the next stop for another train headed in my direction. I would hide in a corner of that station, in case his train crossed the same tracks and he spotted me, abandoning him. I would not suffer his last impression of me to be another act of casual psychoanalysis — another judgment.

I heard a familiar popping sound from my trouser pocket. It was Pound.

'It's the headless guy with the nice bed,' I told Tony. Tony said nothing.

You're closer, now, the headless guy said. *Where are you?*

Coney Island, you?

Same. I'm at Mermaid Avenue and West 44th.

Is that far from Nathan's?

Very close. I can come get you.

'He says he's nearby, and he can host us,' I said. 'He's real close — Mermaid and 44th.'

Tony looked down at the ground and then up into the sky.

'I don't think I can, Sam,' Tony said. 'What would this be tomorrow? Just a haunting, painful thing.'

'We'd have had tonight,' I said. 'All we ever have is tonight.'

'And if I want more?' Tony asked.

'What more is there?' I asked.

'What if I want tomorrow?' Tony asked. 'What if this was supposed to be forever, and you've made a decision I'll never comprehend? Because you've decided to suffer.'

'You're like every man I've ever met, Tony,' I said, tongue of a viper, speaking to slice and dice. 'Either you want nothing much or you want to get married after a few hours together. I'm not stupid like that anymore. I have one night left with a libido. I have to give myself this last moment's pleasure.'

'I also have to be fair to myself,' Tony said.

I had nothing else to say, so I said nothing. Tony's eyes searched mine for something that no longer existed in me. Tony turned and crossed the street into the large, gaping mouth of the Coney Island subway station.

'Goodbye!' I shouted.

I realised he had never offered me his phone number. But what good would his phone number have done me the next day? Maybe we could have been friends, I thought. But I had no gay friends. I either dated the gay men I encountered, had sex with them one or a few times, or wondered why they had not engaged me in either course of action.

Moments later, I continued on my trek along Stillwell Avenue, passing the large Coney Island subway terminal and its closed, dark, empty shops. I felt eyes on me. It was perhaps just my imagination — I have no reason to feel I am psychic. If I could have seen the future, I would not have been there at all. I wondered if the feeling of being watched was Tony, surveying me from one of the subway platforms overhead. Around the time of the *Twilight* series and other such vampire romance fiction, I had begun to imagine that the love of my life had always been watching me, waiting for me to delete Pound and become a more respectable person before he would present himself.

I didn't feel overcome with romance in that moment. The feeling of being watched put a chill in me, like the feeling of an unseen hand gently caressing the back of my neck. I picked up the pace and began to walk with greater purpose in the direction of my final fuck. And then as the disquiet within me grew, I began to run in the direction of Mermaid Avenue. At one point on that road, there was a near-total absence of light. I imagined that there would be someone in the shadows at some point who would make themselves known. That person never appeared. The farther I ran, the more certain I was of the profound stillness that lay ahead.

31. Aircraft الطائرات

'Can I make you something?' Sam(a) asked Ayoub, breaking his silence. She wondered how long he would have sat in silence had she not spoken. She imagined herself spending the rest of her time in Alexandria that way — not seeing the Mediterranean or her ancestors' graves, but waiting for Ayoub to speak.

'Sama, my mother insisted that you stay with us and that we not ask questions, so I asked no questions. We put you up, and we treat you as a daughter of the family,' he said.

Sam(a) looked down at her hands, resting in her lap. She retreated into her hands. Whatever Ayoub had to say could not hurt her there.

'When I come home for lunch and find an empty house, of course I wonder what you could be doing, galavanting about town. I wonder what sort of person you are,' he said.

Sam(a) thought for a second that she could raise to Ayoub that she would never have left the house if it had not been to find his wandering mother. But she would not. Hawa was Sam(a)'s great-great-grandmother and a singular friend in an unsettling place with the distinction of being at once familiar and strange. What's more, Sam(a) was determined not to apologise for leaving the house unsupervised, on principle.

'I see. Mister Ayoub, may I please ask you a question?' Sam(a) asked.

Ayoub offered no more than his silence.

'I only want to better understand you: Is the reason you would have me stay at home that you are afraid of what would happen to me if I went outside?'

'Yes,' Ayoub said. 'The papers are saying it, plain as day: Women are going missing in this neighbourhood. Just today, I read that another girl from Sporting went missing. Can you understand what that means? It means that among us — among the goodly, genteel people going about their day in Cleopatra, there's a kidnapper and probably a killer — or worse — of women. He could be next door. He could be anywhere. Will you understand the gravity of such a thing only when it's too late?'

'I want to understand you, Mister Ayoub,' Sam(a) said. 'Perhaps understanding you would help me understand the gravity of this situation. I want to understand the fear. Is there a fear so great that it merits locking oneself away? Is that sort of life worth saving? A lot of a tiny, little life. What's the point?'

Sam(a)'s questions came from a place of American male arrogance. She wondered in that moment if she would set into motion a series of events that would smash the patriarchy, first in the house on Flower Street, then in Egypt, then in the world. Sam(a) failed to recognise how her questions — which resembled her interviews for her work in journalism — were a kind of amateur psychological practice, the kind she detested. A great many professions resemble a kind of unqualified therapy. Had she known that she was acting as a therapist and that she had been condescending to her ancestor, would she have stopped her line of questioning?

Would she have done an about-face and apologised to Ayoub for leaving the home and become a very quiet person? Or would she have doubled down?

'You don't need to understand me, girl,' Ayoub said, his voice like the rumblings before an earthquake. 'You need to respect that what I say is in the interest of keeping you and the women of this house safe.'

'I really mean you no disrespect,' Sam(a) said, trying to backpedal.

'Of course not. And you will of course not leave the house again without Lilia and Ghozala or a chaperon,' he said. 'It's settled.'

Sam(a) looked down at her hands. She was resolved to leave that evening.

'Please tell me how you are able to do it,' Sam(a) asked, looking up again.

'Do what, child?' he asked.

'To live a lot of a little life,' she said. 'You seem to live so miserably and without complaint.'

'The passing of time will teach you how,' he said.

'What does that mean? Could you please speak as plainly as possible, so that I can understand? If I leave this house knowing the answer to this question, I will have at least earned peace in my heart during my time here.'

'The more you live, the more you see death and suffering all around, the more you realise that you are not owed happiness or to feel entertained,' Ayoub said.

Sam(a) remembered the mysterious death of Ayoub's wife. She wanted to know what had happened to her. She could not bring herself to ask something so forward.

'Please forgive me for prying, but what death have you known, sir?' Sam(a) asked. 'Your parents live in the garden behind your house.'

'My late wife. She was very ill. She suffered greatly,' Ayoub said.

By ill, he means crazy, Sam(a) thought. *Crazy for detesting her husband and wanting to be free of him in the summer heat.*

'Mentally or physically?' Sam(a) asked.

'Both — She died in the pellagra epidemic many years ago,' Ayoub said. 'A problem of nutrition that affects the body and the spirit.'

'Was she angry at you specifically, your wife?' Sam(a) asked, revealing that she knew a bit too much. Ayoub looked at her blankly. 'And why wasn't her anger directed at the others? At the girls and Wassim?'

There was a deafening silence in the kitchen. Sam(a) worried that she was hurting Ayoub. Her heart hurt, empathetically.

'And her death hurt you — and that's why you are afraid of us disappearing?' Sam(a) asked.

'There doesn't need to be a very elegant explanation for me not wanting you to die, Sama,' Ayoub said. 'But if you should require poetry to understand: Know that I have already lost one woman to an unseen killer, yes. You are bored, locked away in this house. I can understand that. And it would of course be wonderful to live in a world where our daughters could walk around freely and without fear of the men who are pigs — and worse — but we do not. Ultimately, none of this will mean anything, in the face of life and death,' Ayoub said.

'But why should I be made to pay for the wrongs of pigs?' Sam(a) returned.

Ayoub tilted his head and raised a hand to the sky. *Heaven knows*, was his meaning. Sam(a) could have pressed him on this question, but she had another: 'And if life is so meaningless, why not encourage me to go out into the streets and enjoy what time I have to be here?'

'Because it is a sin to commit suicide, Sama. We live for as long as we are meant to live. But make no mistake, Sama: None of this life matters. All our caprices — all the boredom and unfulfilled desires and expectations are illusions,' Ayoub said. 'And yet — and this is the riddle of it all — we must keep going, somehow. We must live.'

'Why?' she said, frustrated.

'Why, for Paradise!' Ayoub said. 'If we live well — not in the way you feel entitled to live, but if we live lots of little lives, as you say — then we will meet again, in paradise. Heaven will reward us handsomely for our sorrows, Sama. That's what you should tell yourself when you feel restless at home: I will want for nothing in Paradise!'

Sam(a)'s heart sank. She had lived sinfully in New York. She would not arrive at the Kingdom of which he spoke. Ayoub would, and his wife — whatever enmity there had been between them — would. And Sam(a) would end up somewhere else. There is no inverse of Heaven in Judaism, as there is in the other Arab faiths. So she wondered if she would end up nowhere at all.

'I love you, Mister Ayoub,' Sam(a) said. She had to say it in that moment, since she did not know if she would have a chance to say it after death. Ayoub looked at Sam(a) with wide eyes, a bit frightened.

'Not in an untoward way — I would like for you to know that I feel you are a father to me, and that you are a good and a poetic man,' Sam(a) said. Ayoub looked down, full of grace. Blessed was he among men.

Hawa suddenly appeared at the kitchen entryway.

'Son!' Hawa exclaimed, a bit anxiously.

Sam(a) worried that Hawa would confess to having escaped in order to exonerate Sam(a) and, in doing so, further entrench her reputation among the Saadouns as insane and a burden to the family.

'Yes, mama,' Ayoub said.

'Sama is you!' Hawa ejected.

'I see, mama,' Ayoub said, dismissing her prophecy. Sam(a) wondered if somewhere in Hawa's past, a wicked village witch had condemned her to be a kind of Cassandra.

'Sorry. It occurred to me that I had to say it, so I did,' Hawa said.

'I am also sorry,' Sam(a) said.

The family froze in place for a moment.

Ayoub excused himself from the kitchen. He had to escort Lilia from her typography classes and Ghozala from the hospital. Hawa retreated back to the garden. Sam(a) watched her from the kitchen window, pacing to-and-fro, waltzing with herself. Hawa would meander in the direction of the alleyway and then retreat back to the bushes to inspect them and then retreat back into an inner-dialogue.

Immediately after they were gone, Sam(a) became emboldened by a feeling that she had nothing to lose. She ran to Ayoub's room. She opened his bureau drawer, and in it, beside some stationary and a revolver with a wooden handle was Ayoub's package that had become the object of Sam(a)'s wonderment. Sam(a) undid the twine string around it and gingerly peeled back the flap of the envelope from its adhesive. Tucked inside were pages of stamps in mint condition and a certificate of authenticity from the Alexandria chapter of the Egyptian National Philatelic Society. Some stamps inside an envelope. Nothing more. Sam(a) was overcome with disappointment. She felt she had learned nothing of Ayoub or of the past. Or of herself. Stamps! Days of wondering what Ayoub's little, secret parcel contained, and it was no more than little, bullshit pieces of paper that had become almost irrelevant in Sam(a)'s time, with the advent of digital correspondence.

Among the stamps was a single sheet with the portrait of the current king's father and predecessor, Fouad. But then there were pages and pages of stamps with aircraft. There was one recurring image — a plane flying over the pyramids in Giza that read Egypte - الدولة المصرية and Poste Aerienne - البريد الجوي . This stamp was rendered in a rainbow of colours: violet, purple-grey, carmine rose, greenish blue. Another set of multicoloured stamps was from the International Aviation Congress in Cairo in 1933. These stamps did not even bother to include the pyramids. They bore images of different sorts of blimps.

Sam(a) returned the stamps to their package. She thought on them intermittently for the remainder of the day. At first, they were a symbol of what she was beginning to see as a positively meaningless return to Alexandria. After her resentment had fermented within her, at one point she wondered if Ayoub intended to bring his stamp collection with him to Paradise, in the way that the pharaohs were buried with their treasures. Sometimes the pharaohs were buried along with the graven images of servants — images of the variety forbidden by the faiths that the Egyptians practiced in the 1930s. And then Sam(a) felt sorry for thinking such a coldhearted thing about Ayoub. And then, after that contrition, Sam(a) wondered whether she was so wilfully cruel when it came to Ayoub and his view of life and its inverse, because as Hawa had put it so plainly, Sam(a) was him.

That night, after dinner, as the girls prepared for bed, Lilia remarked that Sam(a) had not yet washed one of her frocks as she had every night and pinned it to a clothesline in their bathroom.

'Monsieur Edouard's has not yet delivered your dress?' Lilia asked, as she sat before a vanity mirror in their bedroom, brushing and braiding her hair before bed, as she did every night.

'They haven't,' Sam(a) said.

'Then it will most certainly come tomorrow,' Lilia said.

Sam(a) nodded. She had already arranged to pick up the dress. Without it, she would have to wear her single remaining dress, dirty from her perspiration from the day's running, until the delivery.

Sam(a) waited for the sound of the bathroom door opening. She had to speak to Ghozala. When she heard the bathroom door open, she shot out into the hallway.

'Doctor Fahmy,' Sam(a) shot at Ghozala in a whisper. Ghozala was visibly startled by the way Sam(a) hurled these words at her.

'Doctor Fahmy, I want to go home,' Sam(a) said, pouring the hushed words forth from her chest.

'Are you quite alright, Sama?' Ghozala asked, her left eye twitching aggressively. 'What's the matter with you?'

'Nothing. Never mind,' Sam(a) said.'I was confused for a moment, but I'm fine now.' In her mind's eye, Sam(a) saw the Saadouns relegating her to the smokey back apartment with Hawa and Adam, another madwoman for their collection, another burden to the family.

Sam(a) excused herself to the bathroom. She looked at herself in the mirror. She touched the mirror to be certain it wasn't a portal back to 21st century New York. It was not. Sam(a) inspected the smudge stain from her fingers on the looking glass. It was nothing more than a smudge stain in the shape of her dainty, little fingerprints.

32. Take My Breath Away

The year of my birth, *Take My Breath Away* by Berlin hit the top of the charts. It became an auspicious song, in my mind. Often, at key moments in my life, it would come on randomly, and I would interpret in it whatever expediency demanded.

One time, getting a haircut in Manhattan's Chinatown, where I often found myself aimlessly wandering in my college days at New York University, the Cantonese version of *Take My Breath Away* by Hong Kong pop star Sandy Lam came on over the radio. My stylist, an older Hong Kongnese American woman with a shock of purple hair, told me to watch a film with that song — Wong Kar-wai's 1988 classic *As Tears Go By*. That began my love affair with Wong's movies, one auspicious event. And then there was another: Based on that song and its film, I decided to apply for a two-month journalism internship at a newspaper in Hong Kong. The paper offered me a job after the internship, but I had to go back to New York. For Wassim, who by then had lost his wife and lived on his own, in a place that never became familiar to him, try as he did to build us a home. I never stood a chance.

Mermaid Avenue was better lit by street-lamps. I stopped running. Still I couldn't shake the feeling that I was being followed. My Pound app popped, and the noise puncturing the ocean wind made me jump.

Are you guys almost here? the headless guy asked.

Yeah, a few blocks away, I responded.

Just me though. Friend had to bail.

No response.

I wondered if the headless guy was disappointed. I had promised him a voyeuristic romp. Now it was just me. I felt guilty. False advertisement. Usually in Pound conversations, everyone's roles were carefully predetermined and clearly iterated — That is to say, we made certain with contractual precision who would top and who would bottom and how — with or without condoms, hard or gentle. They were clear transactions. No surprises. I appreciated the clarity of Pound hookups.

You OK with that — Just you and I? I asked.

Silence.

Sorry for the change of plans, I continued.
Totally fine if you want to call the whole thing off.

Hurry the fuck up man, he answered. *I've been here ready for you.*

On my way.

Building 440 — There are two buzzers. I'm the one on the right.

213

Coming.

I had never been to that end of Mermaid Avenue. Walking toward 44th, still a bit out of breath from my run, I remarked that the neighbourhood was not quite as rough as people said. I passed a closed cupcake shop and an organic food market. And then I heard a groaning sound in the distance just ahead. I passed a young man, propped against a boarded-up construction site, shooting heroin. I made a loop out into the street to avoid him.

'What are you looking at, fuck face?,' the kid shooting heroin ejected.

Finally I arrived at the building, a bit more dilapidated than the others. Above a closed bodega were two windows, one dark and the other with a ruby red light pouring out from under a blackout curtain. I could hear the bass of a slow, almost operatic song pumping through the building's brick exterior. To the side of the bodega was a single door, with a window looking into an unlit staircase leading to the apartments over the shop. I hit the right button on the buzzer. No response. I hit it again. I waited for a minute. I saw the red light from the apartment overhead reflect on the pavement to the side of me. The headless guy must have peaked through his curtains. Then I heard a loud, buzzing noise, signifying that the door was open. I pulled doorknob and entered. It was a heavy door. It closed behind me with a loud thud. When I entered the stairwell, I immediately recognised the song. It was *Take My Breath Away.* The tail end of it. An auspicious song for my last time ever. I could hardly hear myself think. Finally in the moment's silence between *Take My Breath Away* and some

214

house music, full of thumping bass, I heard a loud banging on the plexiglass window of the door behind me. I felt the blood rush to my ears. I turned, certain it was the heroin kid. But it was Tony, looking through the window. He looked like a ghost. The colour had gone from his face, and his eyes were bugging out of his head. I turned to open the door. Tony reached in, took my hand, and pulled me back into the street.

'Are you alright?' I asked, stunned.

Tony was loudly panting. He spoke in between deep, gasping breaths.

'I was standing on the platform... for the subway... The bed' , Tony said. 'He showed you a bed.'

I looked at Tony, collecting my thoughts, and then I realised the headless guy was HOST, who wanted to slice me up. Suddenly, the red light from overhead flooded out into the asphalt below. I couldn't see HOST's face — Just the silhouette of a man, backlit by a powerful red light. And then the silhouette released the blackout curtains again, and the shadow was gone.

My Pound popped.

Coming for you, HOST said.

HOST had made another Pound account. HOST was ready for me. The bed looked too perfect. The bed had been a screenshot from an online furniture catalogue.

A dim, flickering light turned on in the stairwell. And cutting the light in two was the long shadow of the headless HOST man approaching at vertiginous speeds — gliding over the steps like a wildcat chasing its prey.

'Fuck!' I yelled, grabbing Tony's hand back with force. The word 'Fuck!' shot forth from my mouth like a bullet from a revolver. The sound of my heart in my ears matched the sound of the soles of our shoes hitting the pavement as we charged forth, back to Stillwell. We passed back through the darkness beside the Coney Island subway terminal. I no longer had the feeling of being followed. In my frantic thoughts, I turned to Tony. I reckoned it must have been the feeling of Tony following me, after he realised that the headless HOST man was out to slice me.

'We can't stay here waiting for the subway,' Tony said.

'Why not? Let's get the fuck out of here,' I said, catching my breath.

'Those platforms are totally empty, and there's only one exit. And the trains run slower this late at night,' Tony said. There were side entrances to the terminal, one of which led to the dark sidewalk on Stillwell Avenue, but they were shut at night with big iron gates to discourage the poor from living there or jumping the turnstiles. There was a small police station in the terminal at the subway's main entrance, but it was closed, and if we told the police that we were being pursued by a man from a gay sex app, how would they respond, if they did respond?

'Where do we go?' I asked, my mind a blur. The subway was out of the question. Behind us was the amusement park, and beyond that was the Atlantic Ocean, and beyond that was Alexandria.

In the distance, back on Stillwell Avenue, we heard the sound of someone running — shoes hitting the pavement. It could have been anyone, but the street had been so quiet before that moment that the odds were against us. Time was running out.

33. 讓我屏住呼吸 تخطف الانفاس

When her great aunts — that is to say, Lilia and Ghozala, not Doctor Fahmy — were asleep, Sam(a) crept out of bed. Sam(a) changed back from her nightgown into the single frock she owned and descended the stairs quietly from the bedroom to the sitting room downstairs.

Sam(a) had some difficulty seeing without turning on the lights, but the moon was full that night, and its light shone through the windows of the house on Flower Street. A large grandfather clock in the sitting room read that it was nearly 10:30 p.m. She was late. She crept through the dining room to the kitchen, and from the kitchen to a small back room with a door leading out into the garden. For a moment, she stopped in her tracks and looked at the brush at the right of the garden. She wondered if the portal back through her hypnotic entrance into this world opened at night. She had no time to look. Even if it did, she felt she had to say goodbye to Wassim. And at least to Hawa, if not the others.

Suddenly, a light from the kitchen shone on the grass beside her. She looked up into the window. She saw Ayoub inspecting the garden from the kitchen window. She ducked and clung to the back wall of their home. When the light turned out, she breathed a sigh of relief. Sam(a) realised something about escaping the house on Flower Street — that hesitation only gave the Saadouns more opportunity to hear the creaking of floor boards and discover the would-be escapee making off into the night. It is safer to make a resolute run for it than to tip-toe around.

Still ducking, Sam(a) quickly looped around the back of the house and into the alleyway leading out of the garden, there she stood in near-perfect darkness. She saw the the reflection of the moonlight on Flower Street in the distance. Above her, there was the sapphire night sky with clouds so low to the buildings that she felt she could touch them. The clouds recalled to her Chungking Express, another film by Wong Kar-wai, not yet born to his family in Shanghai. She woke herself from her reverie and began her trek through the alley with purpose, guided only by the little light from the sky above and the street ahead.

Halfway through the alleyway, and in one of the narrow passages of her brain, Take My Breath Away began to play. And with that song, she remembered the last night Brighton, which had been several nights prior, in 1930s Alexandria time.

As Sam(a) passed under the archway and onto Flower Street, her pace slowed. The song haunted her. She was still shaken by what had happened on Stillwell Avenue. She thought on Ayoub's prohibition against leaving the house. It had been no more than an old-fashioned Egyptian man's misogyny, she was certain of it. And yet, just as soon as she recalled last night in Brighton and the feeling of Stillwell Avenue, the sensation of being watched not even by a person, but the Heavens, followed her to her tryst on the corniche.

As she approached the two large boulevards before the Mediterranean, Sam(a) found Antoun standing beneath a streetlamp, his face shrouded in the shadows cast upon him by the champagne-coloured light and his fedora. She wondered if she could see his face clearly if he would look as he had that night in the narrow behind the synagogue, or if he would appear as a ghost. She wondered if he was alive somewhere, in the 21st century modern day — if he was someone's ancestor that she was about to ensnare in her Tiresian endeavour.

Still hidden by the shadows of Flower Street, she saw Antoun remove a pocket watch from the vest inside his large coat. Sam(a) watched him standing still in the safety of the shadows. He looked to the West. He saw something there, in the way that cats sometimes seem to look into the darkness and detect prey that is invisible to normal, human eyes. A moment later, Antoun turned and began to stroll slowly Westward on the corniche. Sam(a) felt as though she should run after him, but Take My Breath Away would not allow it. Last night in Brighton would not allow it. Her feet were planted on Flower Street. Perhaps it was Ayoub — the Ayoub in her — that forbid her passage.

Sam(a) watched Antoun amble about a quarter mile up the corniche. She saw the little shadow of a woman, standing up against a lamplight, smoking. Antoun approached her. A moment later, he rested his hand above her on the street lamp. Sam(a) spied some movement between the two — a transaction. Then they ran — or skipped, rather — together, Antoun's arm around the woman's shoulders, southward toward Borg el Arab. And like that, Antoun disappeared into the night — and from Sidi Gaber and from Sam(a)'s consciousness —like all the vanished girls in the papers.

Sam(a) recoiled into the darkness, defeated. Travelling up Flower Street, she still couldn't shake the feeling of being followed. She passed the would-be Chili's. There was nothing but darkness in the alley beside the Saadoun home that led back to the garden from whence she came. The Flower Street flower shop was closed.

Sam(a) turned onto Tigran Basha. Ramzi's shawarma shop was still open. The radio was on, a bit lower than before — an unfamilar song. The rarely seen Ramzi stood behind the service counter. Sam(a) hadn't made any noise audible beyond the static sound of the wind blowing inland from the sea. But as she passed, Ramzi, a pallid and gaunt man with a handlebar moustache, looked at her, his eyes glued to her as though he had seen a ghost or an exotic animal passing through the street before his shop.

Finally, when Sam(a) arrived on Sidi Gaber, she remarked how an area she had only seen crowded with frenzied men coming to and from the tram was now totally empty, save a couple of stray cats. They were mating, she thought. But she could not be sure, since cat intercourse often sounds like violence.

Not wanting to cause a stir late at night, Sam(a) gently tapped on a glass pain at the Monsieur Edouard shop door. A moment later, Ilyas opened the door and bid Sam(a) enter. Ilyas was wearing only an under shirt with suspenders holding up his trousers. He looked dapper, Sam(a) thought.

'I've been waiting for you,' Ilyas said, escorting her inside the fitting room, dimly lit as before. 'Your dress has been ready for your since the afternoon.'

'I'm very sorry. I could only make it out just now,' Sam(a) said.

'I see. No one saw you leaving, of course?' Ilyas asked.

Sam(a) said nothing. Ilyas stopped and looked Sam(a) in the face, as if he was ready to give her a spanking. 'Naughty girl,' he said, with a faint smile, disappearing behind the black curtains that separated the fitting room from the back room.

'Where is Mister Hani?' Sam(a) asked, standing on the pedestal at the centre of the fitting room. She waited, perched awkwardly on the stand, for Ilyas to retrieve her dress. Non-Arab classical music played lightly from a radio in the back room. Tchaikovsky, None but the lonely heart.

'Probably home asleep by now,' Ilyas said, returning from the back room with Sam(a)'s dress, casually draped over one arm.

'Change,' he said.

'Right here?' Sam(a) asked.

'Right here,' he said.

Sam(a) thought on her Tiresian endeavour and then that Ilyas was not unhandsome. She undid the buttons at the front of her dress and pulled her arms out from inside of it, until it fell to the pedestal below, revealing only her body and her underwear.

'You have healthy curves,' Ilyas said. 'One cannot tell when you're clothed — When you're clothed, you look scrawny.'

Sam(a) wondered if this had been a compliment. She stepped into the deep red dress and pulled it up over her shoulders. It fit snuggly, like a second-skin.

'It's a bit tight,' Ilyas said. He hopped up onto the pedestal, startling Sam(a). Ilyas's abdomen touched Sam(a)'s. Ilyas embraced Sam(a), his arms reaching around her. She embraced him back. And looking downward over his shoulder, she saw a pair of cloth sheers in his back pocket. So quickly that Sam(a) felt herself almost too stunned to react, Ilyas reached back and grabbed the sheers. Sam(a) reflexively kneed Ilyas in the crotch. He stumbled back down from the pedestal.

Suddenly, they heard a loud rapping at the door. Both froze in place for a moment. Sam(a) wondered if there was a back exit. The loud rapping repeated. Ilyas peeked behind the scarlet modesty curtains that blocked the voyeurs of Sidi Gaber. Sam(a) worried that Ilyas would shew the caller away — that whoever had come to call would not see her in the murderer's lair. But somehow, by the grace of Heaven, Ilyas opened the door and preceded to step backward. Into the fitting room was a ghostly mass of black cloth behind a long, cowboy revolver with a wooden handle.'

'Put the sheers on the floor right where you are and go sit over there, you dog and son of dogs,' Hawa said, pointing with the revolver to the loveseat where Lilia and Ghozala sat days before. 'And don't do anything smart. You don't want to find out how clever I can be.'

Ilyas did as he was told. Sam(a) leapt down from the pedestal and gestured for Hawa to hand her the gun. With a force, Hawa used the gun to push Sam(a) aside.

'I can manage,' Hawa told Sam(a). 'Watch.'

'You're the one disappearing our girls,' Hawa said. مش كده؟ - Mish kida? - Isn't that so?

Ilyas looked at her, stunned.

'I can hear you thinking of charging at us, Ilyas — Bad idea,' Hawa said, an expression like Gloria Swanson's in the last scene of Sunset Boulevard. 'I am the Madwoman of Flower Street, and I will take from you your manhood and leave you alive to watch it happen, understand? Don't make a single move. I can hear the thoughts in your frantic, pinched head,' Hawa said. 'Good boy. Now I want to know why you are like this — a butcher of women.'

'Because I am a butcher of women,' Ilyas said. 'How did you figure it out?'

'I've seen you at your new store in Sporting, where the last woman went missing,' Hawa said. 'We have a house full of young women, so I watch from the shadows. I spend my life wandering and watching. And when I saw this one come to you late at night, I knew for certain it was you.'

'Very clever,' Ilyas said.

'And you have cleverly sidestepped my question, Ilyas — Why are you a butcher of women? And where are they?' Hawa said.

'You should know,' Ilyas said with a solemn expression and a raised brow.

Hawa pointed her gun at Ilyas's crotch. 'A lesson for you, son: You are in no position for jokes and riddles. Don't try my patience.'

Ilyas lifted a palm to Hawa and cleared his throat. 'First, you should know that I've never met Monsieur Edouard in my life,' Ilyas began. 'He is a man who communicates with me through go-betweens, like fortunetellers help people communicate with spirits. Just as Hani and I started emerging from the lean times of the Depression, and just as he gave us a new boutique in Sporting, he began to open a series of other stores, all in the same area. I tried to speak to his people for weeks — to explain that his franchise was driving our revenue into the ground and that he was competing with himself and pulling us under in the process. Nothing. No response. I became desperate.'

'The girls,' Hawa said.

'Hani's cousin Ramzi supplies meat to the other vendors on Tigran Basha, wholesale,' Ilyas said.

'Heaven forgive you, Ramzi,' Hawa said.

Sam(a) feared that something was lost in translation. She did not follow.

'Cleopatra has been eating its own flesh!' Hawa said. 'All those young women, gone so you could make ends meet for Monsieur Edouard.'

'Not all,' Ramzi said. 'Three of the eight women the press has identified, Hani and I lured and killed. Sama would have been the fourth of nine — Like Monsieur Edouard's dressmakers, we aren't the only game in town.'

Sam(a) wondered how this would end.

'Ilyas, get on your knees,' Hawa said.

Ilyas did as asked. He began to weep.

'Is there nothing more important to you than making ends meet?' Hawa asked.

'Nothing — What life do I have, other than trying to stay afloat here?' Ilyas said.

Hawa pressed the revolver to his forehead.

'And to do that, you sacrifice our own?' Hawa said. 'Imagine all the suffering you've caused.'

'I'm so sorry! Heaven forgive me. I'm so sorry! Kill me please! Please end it!'

'If I hear another woman goes missing in Cleopatra, or

in Sporting, you'll wish I'd have killed you,' Hawa said, eyes drilling into his. 'Sama, get your things. Say goodbye to Mister Ilyas.'

'Goodbye, Mister Ilyas,' Sam(a) said in a stupor.

Hawa took Sam(a) by the wrist as they left. Hawa said nothing. She held Sam(a)'s arm as they passed Ramzi's on Tigran Basha. The light in the shop was still on, and Ramzi stood together with Hani. Hawa stopped and pointed her gun in the direction of Sidi Gaber.

'Your Mister Ilyas has a message for you,' she said.

As they continued onto Flower Street, Sam(a) heard the sound of shoe soles beating the pavement. She turned and saw Hani running in the direction of Sidi Gaber. Ramzi stood before his shop, watching Hawa and Sam(a) as they turned the corner. Hawa squeezed Sam(a)'s arm tightly as a sign to her not to look back.

On Flower Street, Sam(a) whispered to her great-great-grandmother, 'Should we go to the police?'

Hawa said nothing.

'You're going to leave them like that? What if they do it again?' Sam(a) said.

'Then they'll all have their place in my garden,' Hawa said. 'You understand?'

'What about the families of the girls they've murdered?' Sam(a) said. 'Don't they deserve justice?'

'Don't be naive, Sama,' Hawa said. 'The police don't resolve things for everyday people. And there's no proof. We've eaten it all.'

Sam(a) recalled that there was no forensic testing, no security cameras. It was the word of the legendary Phantom of Flower Street and her boarder from Mansoura against businessmen.

'Heaven awaits us all, Sama. Heaven will judge us all,' she said. 'As for the rest of the missing women, in my mind they left their homes, saw the world, and lived wildly. Better lives than you or I could ever imagine. Weightless lives.'

They passed through the alley in the darkness. Sam(a) looked up, and there were no longer any clouds. That is what it is to live by the sea: The weather changes in an instant. She could see the cosmos from the narrow alleyway beside the Saadoun house on Flower Street .

In the garden, she asked Hawa, 'And what about me?'

'What about you, stupid girl?' Hawa said.

'I will also be judged?' Sam(a) asked.

'Whatever brought you to that shop in the middle of the night, my daughter— Heaven holds more compassion and mercy than you or I can fathom,' she said. 'Beyond your wildest imagination. If I'm compassionate enough to forgive you your trespasses, it would be a shame to think Heaven would not, isn't it so?'

34. Last Train Out of Brighton

Tony and I bolted out of the subway terminal onto Surf Avenue and from there we turned into a side street.

We stopped just past the street corner, calculating where to go and catching our breaths. I turned to look back at Surf Avenue. No one was there.

On the side street, the lights were on — lots of old Las Vegas show bulbs — but everyone had gone home. With the sound of the wind blowing in from the ocean, it felt like a biblical sort of end, like this had once been a street teaming with life, and then like in one of the magic shows they performed there, everyone was gone without a trace. I was startled by the sound of a large rat coming up for air in a rubbish bin full of half-eaten cotton candy and hot dogs. A billboard just above Tony advertised a bearded lady and a sword-swallower.

Across from the sideshow were a series of quarter machines. These were shows with mechanised mannequins that, when prompted by a coin, would sway to-and-fro or lift and lower an arm to the tune of old songs. One of the mannequins was a young girl, clasping her hands like a dope. Hand-painted with calligraphic flourishes beneath her was the title of her song — *Will You Still Love Me Tomorrow?* These were glorified jukeboxes, I thought. The other mannequins — old witches, pied pipers, a suggestive-looking fish — all stared, their eyes frozen on us. Judgment Day came at around 1 a.m. in Coney Island. We ran through the labyrinth of mannequins and onto the boardwalk. I kept looking back, and there was no one.

We walked with purpose along the planks of the boardwalk to Brighton Beach. A few people passed us, leaving the area's festivities. We passed the falafel stand again, closed now.

'Delete Pound,' Tony said.

I didn't ask why.

'So the guy can't track you,' he said. 'Do what you want later, but for now, delete it.'

Still en route toward Brighton, I took out my phone and deleted my Pound for the first time in a decade since I first discovered it existed. I had been through several phones since then — many lost or cracked, but I had always been in the position of downloading or updating it. It had simply never occurred to me to delete it. In 2011, I thought it was liberating and honest. Sex is always transactional — as loving as it can seem. That would be true long after that night. At least in America. At least for me.

We passed through an alleyway onto Brighton Beach Avenue. From there, we climbed two flights of stairs to the elevated subway platform running along all the post-Soviet attractions we had seen earlier that night. This was farewell. I had seen the last of Brighton Beach. After hypnotherapy, I would book a flight to Egypt and find some way to busy myself until I joined my family's dust.

'I'm sorry,' I said. 'I'm embarrassed. To say the least.'

'What do you mean?' Tony asked.

'To have dragged you down with me,' I said.

A moment passed. The sound of the ocean calmed us.

'Then if you're sorry, you owe me,' Tony said. 'Don't go tomorrow. Don't castrate yourself with hypnosis. If it's an actual thing and not just some ridiculous scam, then it's a miserable idea, all the same. It doesn't matter if you don't want to be with me. I'm not saying this because I like you. I'm saying, stop mutilating yourself.'

I said nothing.

'It's not what you want,' Tony said. 'You don't want to be less whole, Sam. You wouldn't spend so much time thinking about life if you didn't want to be well. I speak to a lot of people who want to end things. You aren't those people, Sam. You're too invested. You think of a future.'

'I want to be able to want you, Tony. I want to be able to recognise that I want you and to not be alone. And to not just want you because I am alone. And for me not to give up everyone else to be with you for a few years, before you realise that I weigh too much in whatever sense — figurative or literal — and then you bounce. Imagine if things were so easy for me, we'd have met tonight, and we'd have dated, instead of me almost getting us killed so I could have sex one last time.'

Tony was silent.

'See — You don't want to be it for me,' I said. 'Who would? All I have is what's passed.'

'If you think the past is a better bet, sorry to break it to you, Sam, but you're sorely mistaken,' Tony said. 'I'm here. I'm here for you. Right now. I'm ready to do this. I'm so here for you I've followed you all over Brighton fucking Beach. I almost got myself killed saving your ass, Sam.'

'You're upset,' I said. 'If you're frustrated now, what would our lives be like, together?'

'Of course I'm fucking upset!' he exclaimed. 'I don't know what more to say to get you to live. With me or alone.'

The wind roared on the subway overpass. It assaulted the ears. I wanted to hug Tony. But I could not bring myself to use his body for warmth. The train finally approached.

'I can't do this to you for however long you'd have me,' I said. 'Drag you down into the grave with me.'

The subway arrived. I followed Tony toward the open doors. And then the best solution for him presented itself. I let them close between us. Tony turned, shock in his face. I touched the plexiglass. I caressed the glass that kept me from his beautiful face as it sped off toward the city.

As I waited for the next subway, I sat on a wooden bench in plain view of the Atlantic Ocean nestled between flat blocks, the roaring winds battering my body. I thought to leave the subway station and walk to Egypt. Just keep walking until I reached Egypt. Tony had said that I had not wanted to go to Egypt in the modern day. The winds roared, boxing my ears. I lost my fleeting thoughts in the winds.

By the time I got back to the Lower East Side, I had just enough time to get a coffee from a corner bodega and hop on an R train to Bay Ridge. The subway car was empty. Most people head in the other direction, toward Manhattan, at that hour. The passage through the tunnels felt ceremonious. There are people who live down here, I thought. I had often heard legends of the eccentrics who choose to live underground, in the subway system. I had never seen any of them. I watched my own reflection in the subway windows as

I traveled from Manhattan to Brooklyn, to Doctor Fahmy's office.

When I arrived, I explained to Doctor Fahmy that I did not want to inhibit my sexuality.

'I am not a sex addict,' I said. 'I just wanted to be something — someone else.' I told her that I thought it would make Egypt easier for me if I returned without being gay.

'I understand,' she said.

'I thought you might' , I replied.

I told her about Tony. I told her about Egypt and how he said that Egypt today is not the answer. That I wanted to go back in time. I told her that I wanted her to put peace in my heart, however she could.

'You have unresolved issues with the past,' she said.

I nodded.

'I can take you there,' she said.

Doctor Fahmy explained that she could alter her past-life regression therapy. I immediately agreed. I told her to name her price. I had anticipated that she would offer me something like this — something only another Egyptian could know to offer.

'You think I'm bullshitting you,' she said.

I did.

'I'm here, aren't I? I paid upfront,' I replied. I wanted to sound confident in my decision, but I had not slept the night before and my feet were tired. I wanted to spread my toes, but my shoes were full of sand. I hoped she would not notice little grains of sand on her wooden floors. I reckoned I looked like a ghost — or worse, a drug addict — large, puffy circles under my eyes. But then again, maybe she was used to this class of people — the ghost and/ or junkie class of half-living people.

'Because if you actively disbelieve it, it won't work,' she continued. 'Because I can't guarantee your satisfaction.'

'What does that mean?' I asked, a bit worried.

'It means that if you don't get there, that's on you,' she answered — intent, motherly eyes. 'No refunds.'

I looked her in the face. She had a strange twitch. Like a nervous little seizure in her left eye, almost imperceptible.

35. Fun House

Sam(a) woke to the sound of a farmworker calling out his oratory advertisements in the streets. 'It's the last of the oranges,' the farmworker said. 'The oranges are leaving. Farewell, oranges!'

Sam(a) thought nothing of it. She was waiting for the summer — for mango season.

Wassim had promised to take Lilia, Ghozala, and Sam(a) to Parque el-Negoum that day, on the outskirts of town. Ayoub would not come. It did not bear asking. They all knew that Ayoub would be at the synagogue, reciting psalms, as he did everyday. He would come home in the early afternoon, have a small sandwich and a glass of water, and return.

That morning, Hawa meandered about her garden. She saw Sam(a) looking at her through the window, and for the first time in all of Sam(a)'s days in Alexandria in the 1930s, she saw Hawa smile. Hawa smiled and nodded at Sam(a). Sam(a) smiled and nodded, in response. Hawa returned to her meandering. Sam(a) dried the bowl she had just washed from which she had eaten ful medammes for breakfast. She looked up again through the window over the sink. Hawa was gone. Sam(a) figured that Hawa had gone either up the alley into the street and to the sea or back into the little hot box apartment with Adam or through the unknowable portal in the bush at the border of the garden to New York in

2021, where she was a regular, mysterious, and much-adored fixture at a series of underground, femme dance parties called R.Q.S. There, she wore sunglasses, a face mask, and black tracksuit. She frequently requested Warda remixes or glitter pop Beach House ballads in her thick Egyptian accent, and she would sway on the smokey dance floor like a reed in the Nile.

They took a bus. For the first time, Sam(a) saw the Citadel of Qaitbey — small, compact, and robust — and the Abul Abbas al Moursi Mosque, covered in scaffolding, minarets still under construction. From the south of the town, the girls crammed into the back of a taxi together with a woman and her child. Wassim sat up front with the driver and the woman's husband. Sam(a) recognised the South of Alexandria. She reckoned that somewhere along the road, decades later, some city planner would build a Greek-themed city gate with toll booths and the name of the city written in Arabic and Greek atop grandiose columns. And then a municipal transportation minister or some other such official would build an airport just out of reach of Alexandria. And a young Alexandrian American would find that to be a cruel and unexpected coincidence.

Sam(a) looked at Wassim in the front seat and contemplated the barrier between them. Even in time travel or whatever enduring fantasy this had been, cruel and unexpected coincidences separated them.

Parque el-Negoum was crowded that day. A great many Alexandrian men had thought to bring their families to the newly opened amusement park. An Italian-Egyptian entrepreneur, Tommaso Gigliotti, who was born in Cairo, recalled the fanfare surrounding a similar amusement park in the Cairo suburb of Heliopolis, Luna Park — one in a worldwide franchise emanating from Coney Island, Brooklyn — that had long since become defunct. Signore Gigliotti was a whimsical and sentimental man. Rather than try to contact the relevant businesspeople in Brooklyn to propose the construction of a new Luna Park outside of Alexandria, Signore Gigliotti took matters into his own hands and created a near-replica of his childhood paradise and called it Parque el-Negoum - Park of the Stars. Its centrepiece was a large ferris wheel at its centre, a few meters taller than any building in Alexandria at that time. From any given point in the park, one could hear the screams of demure women as the ferris wheel turned and stopped, wooden planks creaking and wrought iron clattering.

Wassim and Lilia waited in the long line for the ferris wheel while Sam(a) and Ghozala entered a building reading in English: *Fun House*. A man in Ancient Egyptian garb — lines drawn emerging from his eyes to make them resemble those on the frescoes found in the pyramids — took their tickets. Inside the Fun House was a maze of mirrors. Ghozala was delighted; she skipped through the maze, laughing and making faces at herself that Sam(a) found to be oddly childish and bordering on insanity, but then, Sam(a) thought, Ghozala had never been jaded by the constant entertainment and desensitisation to joy of modern society. For Ghozala, who had never seen a YouTube video of a cat inadvertently playing a piano with its nonchalant, little paws, her own face was an amusement.

Sam(a) beheld herself with little interest. Sam(a) trailed behind Ghozala who ran ahead making absurd faces at herself in the mirrors. Sam(a) was almost embarrassed at how grotesque Sam(a) seemed to look, stretched and squeezed into hideous and ridiculous shapes — fuzzy, blurry, rotund, inhuman. Sam(a) wanted to leave the Fun House and wait in line with Wassim and Lilia for the ferris wheel.

'Ghozala!' Sam(a) called out, trying to announce her departure from the Fun House. Sam(a) repeated the call once more, a little more loudly the second time, but there was no answer. Sam(a) began to weave through the mirrors only to find more mirrors, contorting her body, until even the strange shape she had taken in Alexandria of the 1930s became unrecognisable to her.

'Ghozala!' she yelled. No one came for her. Not Ghozala, not the Ancient Egyptian attendant who had taken their tickets.

Sam(a) ran to-and-fro. She tried to return to the start of the Fun House, but after a few times running in circles, she realised she was lost. She had entered of her own accord, but now she felt she had passed a point of no-return. Sometimes smoking pot was like this for Sam(a), back in New York. She had wanted to be out of control only until it became upsetting.

In another room, she saw only herself: The room was full of many, small mirrors that reflected a more-or-less normal view of her own face. She had become a Lernaean Hydra from the same myths as Tiresias. She could not bear to see herself this way. She passed to the next room which had mirrors positioned in such a way that she could not see her own reflection at all. She was frightened by this too. There was no state of being or absence that could calm her. And then suddenly, past a passageway to the next room, a familiar head poked out as if to frighten her. It was none other than Doctor Fahmy, smiling ear-to-ear. And then, still smiling, Doctor Fahmy winked, did an about face, and ran away. Already dazzled by the many sights of herself, Sam(a) was stunned.

'Doctor Fahmy!' Sam(a) shouted. Doctor Fahmy's facial expression had frightened Sam(a), so Sam(a) hesitated for a moment and then chased Doctor Fahmy into the next room and the next. Sam(a) was so fixated with catching Doctor Fahmy, always a room ahead, until Sam(a) paid no mind to the strange distortions of her body, which she saw out of the periphery of her sight. Finally, the Fun House expelled Sam(a) out of its backside through a door.

'Doctor Fahmy!' Sam(a) shouted again. The passersby turned to look her up and down. Sam(a) did not care. She turned back to the Fun House, ready to return to the mirrors and find Doctor Fahmy and her way back to whatever present or future tense was on the other side. But there was no doorknob on Fun House back exit. She stood at the door, contemplating which of her realities was reality. This thought was l ike the sensation free-fall she had felt on the ferris wheel with Tony the night before. She thought of Tony. She thought of his face in the moment she let the express Q train pull him from her. Tony looked panicked when Sam(a) caressed the plexiglass between their faces. She had done the only noble and selfless deed of a life spent feeling sorry for her solitude, she thought. She had freed him from the weight of what their intimacy would have been.

Sam(a) beat her fists against the sealed backdoor of the Fun House. Her hands were swollen, she thought. Maybe they had become bloated from the salt and fibre of the ful medammes she had eaten for breakfast. She looked down. She was wearing trousers. On the floor beside her was a tarboush. She felt her chest. Gone were the small breasts. She was wearing a fine three-piece suit, under which she was perspiring.

'What does this mean!' she cried out, exasperated.

More passersby slowed to look at her and quickly hurried along. Sam(a) collected herself and her tarboush from the floor before the onlookers alerted the authorities. She ran to the ferris wheel.

Inching toward the front of the line were Wassim, Ghozala, and Lilia.

'Sami!' Lilia called out. 'You look disheveled. You're a handsome young man, you have to respect yourself, so you can command respect.' Lilia stood on her tiptoes to place the tarboush that Sam(i) had been holding atop his head. She pulled his collar out of his tie, which she then patted down.

Sam(i) looked down at Lilia. He had never seen her from that angle before. He felt the love vibrating through her fingers. He had not known her to be capable of such softness.

'Ghozala — What happened back there?' Sam(i) asked.

'Back where?' Ghozala asked.

Sam(a) said nothing.

When they arrived at the front of the line, a male ride attendant dressed as a bride — overdone makeup with lace and chiffon cascading from head to toe — escorted the Saadouns into their ferris wheel compartments. First the bride escorted the ladies into a compartment, and then he escorted Wassim and Sam(i) into the following compartment. Each compartment was no more than an oversized painted wooden bench for two with a metal bar serving as a safety barrier. They sat motionless for several minutes, and they were off.

'To the stars with you!' the Negoum bride said as they took flight.

Sam(i) was shocked by the sound of the ferris wheel's apparatus churning away to leverage their bodies into the air, only to suspend them there, legs dangling in the sky. Lilia and Ghozala joined their shrieks to the other women on the machine. Wassim and Sam(i) held their breath, such that the shrieks turned inward, coiled within them like sticks of incense, and lived there, gathering mass. Sam(i)'s palms were sweating. He was embarrassed to reveal to Wassim that he was frightened. Under the administrations of the last kings of Egypt under the British, there were a great many government industries and laws and law enforcement with different sorts of applications for different sorts of people. But Sam(i) wondered in that moment if there had been any safety standard set for places like Parque el-Negoum, which was a cheap approximation of the original and probably would have been a trademark infringement in what may — or may not — have been Sam(i)'s modern day. Sam(i) opened his eyes and turned to Wassim. Wassim had also been closing his eyes.

'You're closing your eyes!' Sam(i) remarked, laughing.

'You were also closing your eyes, big guy!' Wassim said, smiling, his eyes still shut tight.

Sam(i) shut his eyes again. All he could hear was the sound of the wind and an occasional scream from the women and children of the ferris wheel. He felt sweat accumulate between his palms and the metal bar that tucked them into the chair.

'Talk to me,' Wassim said with a chuckle. 'About anything other than great heights.'

Sam(i) searched his mind. He had longed for such an opportunity until it presented itself, and now he felt nothing but speechlessness and fear. It was still as it had been when there was a barrier between them posed by gender. And then the right words came to him:

'Alright, but it will be a bit of a mind puzzle for you,' Sam(i) said.

'Try me,' Wassim said.

'Try to imagine that we were father and son,' Sam(i) said. Sam(i) opened his eyes for a moment to look at Wassim, whose eyes were still closed tightly. Sam(i) wanted to know if Wassim would laugh or make any sort of expression of interest when Sam(i) said this. Wassim did not. Wassim sat, eyes closed.

'Is that it?' Wassim asked — 'That I'm your son, or you are my son?'

'I am your son,' Sam(i) said.

'Alright, and?' Wassim asked.

Sam(i) did not know how to continue. Suddenly the ferris wheel's machinations turned. He heard feminine, youthful screams of fear and delight. If he allowed his mind to go fuzzy, they sounded like cheering.

'Imagine I had done something that you would find detestable — That I was born in a way you could not understand, and that there was nothing I could do to make myself a good son for you,' Sam(i) said.

'What do you mean?' Wassim asked. 'Detestable?'

'Imagine that my body was born with some quality you would hate,' Sam(i) said. 'Something against our religion — against Heaven.'

'Yes, O.K.,' Wassim said.

'What would you say?' Sam(i) asked.

'I would say that it is a sin to think that Heaven would make anything detestable' , he said.

'What if you would consider what I had done to be a choice?' Sam(i) said. 'What if I had said or done something you considered to be against our faith?'

'Was it a choice?' Wassim asked.

'What is a choice? I could choose to live miserably or do something I fear to have been against Heaven because I was born wanting — or needing —things you couldn't understand,' Sam(i) said.

'I'm afraid I don't understand,' Wassim said.

Sam(i) felt a bit desperate and then defeated.

'Up, up, and to the stars with you!' Sam(i) heard the ferris wheel bride say, down below. The machinations of the ferris wheel began yet again, setting off the sounds of creaks and clamps and feminine and youthful screams.

'I would love my son,' Wassim said.

The ferris wheel turned again. This time it unsettled Sam(i). It seemed to have moved at regular intervals before. Now it was moving with greater frequency and faster.

'What if that son had done something to bar himself from heaven, and you couldn't be together again, after the Day of Judgment?' Sam(i) asked.

'Heaven is clement, Sami. More than you and I could know. If I can love my son, is it not a sin to presume that Heaven cannot?' Wassim said.

'But we don't know for certain that Heaven is clement?' Sam(i) asked, 'So what if you never saw your son again?'

Sam(i) suddenly heard a familiar voice.

'10...9...8,' it said. Sam(i) immediately recognised it as Doctor Fahmy's voice. The time was near.

'Faith is faith. All we have for certain is now, Sam(i),' Wassim said.

'Up, up, and to the stars with you!,' the ferris wheel bride said, somewhere in the distance. The ferris wheel spun like a rollercoaster. Sam(i) did not dare to open his eyes. He felt his tarboush fall from his head, down to an unseen end. He reached beside himself for Wassim's hand. They held each other's hands tightly. The sounds of feminine and youthful screaming sounded like shouts of adoration.

'7...6...5,' Doctor Fahmy said. Her voice came from above, from somewhere ahead, looking back.

Sam(i) opened his eyes to look at Wassim. He wanted the last thing he saw there to be Wassim. When he opened his eyes, there was only blackness. He saw his own face, black pupils, black sclera.

'Rouhi,' he heard a voice echo in the distance. He felt his palm, empty.

'3...2...1,' Doctor Fahmy said.

Doctor Fahmy excused herself to go to the washroom. The

session had run a bit long, she said. When she returned, she found that Sam(i) had left. She looked out the window to see if she could find him in the street, but he was already well on his way to the subway out of Bay Ridge.

36. Tomorrow‏بكرة - كمان وكمان‏

I had not anticipated I would return to Brighton Beach. Ever. But I felt I had to take the express train that same night out of Manhattan, to Coney Island. For all the times I had gone to Brighton Beach, I never really understood the trains: Sometimes the majority of my ride to the Coney Island terminal ran underground, sometimes it ran overground, and I could see all of Brooklyn. That evening, it was the overground train. From a distance, I could see the Sunset Park Chinatown — one of several in the city. A friend born in China told me that the Sunset Park Chinatown looks nothing like a real Chinese city; it looks like a second-tier Chinese town in the 1980s, she said. I would not know. I've never seen China, and I was too young to know anything of the 1980s.

I crossed Surf Avenue onto Stillwell and made for the boardwalk. I was there for the ferris wheel. All along the subway ride to Coney Island, I recalled what my great-great-grandmother Hawa had said when I first set foot in the house on Flower Street: 'Brookli' and 'Over the moon.' I wondered if by saying this, Hawa had prefigured that I would find Tony in Brooklyn, over Luna — moon — Park.

'Up, up, and to the stars with you,' I thought, as I took off. The park was nowhere near as busy as it had been the previous night. I inspected the seats ahead of me. I turned and saw the seats behind me. I looked down at the ground. I would have known Tony, even from afar. I would have known his hair, his gait. There was no sign of him. As I came back down to Earth, I accepted that the ferris wheel — although a thrill for someone with my particular relationship to heights — was not a magical apparatus, and Hawa was no soothsayer witch or phantom of Flower Street. She was a woman who learned late in life — sooner than many — to live as she pleased and to move without hesitation.

Don't worry, I realised it was my fault that I had let Tony go. But I feel until now it was the right thing to do.

I ambled up the boardwalk, past the falafel shop. Somewhere in the back of my mind was a pain that will never go away. And if I were to linger there, I know it would begin to shred me from the inside. But I was able to continue onward without paying it too much mind.

I continued along the boardwalk until I hit the Soviet-looking flat blocks. For years, the sight of them stirred my senses. But that was yesterday. The apartment complexes were still large and imposing structures — and still architecturally impressive. They were still home to a great many people in the situation of choosing — or falling into — another time and place. But on that evening, the buildings were no more than a reminder to me of a time when they made me feel something other than the void inside me. I thanked the Brighton Beach apartment complexes in the way that Marie Kondo says we should thank our old belongings for their service. There was something still there. But our time so chronically together had come to a close.

Walking along Brighton Beach Avenue, I found that almost all of it had lost its flavour for me. The life had gone from the Anadyr Art and Souvenir's mannequins. Ludmila stared out the shop window. She was as unenthusiastic as she had always been. I had no desire to go to the boardwalk to take in a Russian dinner show. There was no procession of faithful Russian Orthodox people out on the side streets. I returned to Kashkar Cafe. That was all that truly remained for me in Brighton, dumplings and intestine sausages.

I went back to Kashkar Cafe a great many nights. I found that for me, the food is better sober. That's not to judge people who like to get high and stuff their faces. Rather, it's to say that I have discovered myself to be the sort of person who must face life as it is given, without help or hesitation. I have to be certain that I taste what I am eating fully. Or what's the point?

A few weeks later, while I was eating my intestines, Tony walked into Kashkar Cafe. I was certain someone would walk in after him, and that I would have deserved it. He was alone. He nodded and smiled at me as he entered. He ordered his own set of dumplings and a plate of intestines. He said nothing to me. I understood.

I had slowed the pace of my eating to match his. It was a slow night at Kashkar, so the waiter sat him diagonal from me. I realised it would perhaps be the last time I would see him, so I looked at him whenever he looked down at his food. Somewhere in the part of my brain that produces vivid memories, I imagined that we were on a date, that our meal together was intentional. Planned. I wondered if he was imagining the same thing. I excused myself to the bathroom. In the mirror, I fixed my hair and straightened my shirt. I recalled that my great aunt

Lilia had said that one has to respect themselves to be respected.

When I returned to the dining room, Tony was gone. I bolted to the cashier and pulled out my wallet.

'A man paid for you,' the cashier said.

I ran out into the street. I looked both ways. He was gone. My heart sank. I was to blame, yet again. The moment I saw him, I should have gone up to him and sat not even across from but beside him and declared I would never leave.

'Sam,' Tony said, startling me. He had been standing beside the restaurant. He had seen me frantically searching for him. I was embarrassed that he knew how much I wanted him.

'Want to show me around Brighton Beach?' Tony said.

'Not particularly,' I said.

'Well fuck you then,' Tony said, smiling .

'At my place,' I said.

'What about the hypnosis?' he asked.

It was our second date. I had already shown Tony the absolute worst of myself. I would not tell him about Alexandria in the 1930s.

'I want you,' I said. 'If that matters to you anymore.'

'Maybe someday,' Tony said. 'Not tonight.'

We walked along Brighton Beach Avenue. There was a distance between us. On occasion our bodies collided, and then we'd resume our normal course of ambling. We passed the fortuneteller from the night before. Tony had insisted the previous night that we enter. Then we passed Skovorodka, where we had dessert — cherry dumplings, Napoleon cake, and some coffee. Neither of us suggested that we stop for dessert. At any point, we could have ascended the long staircases to the subway overpass that had returned us to our homes the night before.

To my left, a few meters away, I passed a rotund woman with a short, bouffant hairdo. She wore a bright red shirt from one of the Brighton discount clothing shops over pistachio-green jeans. She smoked a long, thin lady cigarette, back against the wall. She looked up at the subway overpass that was the bane of her existence. I wondered if I had woken her the previous night, when I finally left Brighton. I did not yawn. I did not need her sort of release that night. I moved on.

At the end of Brighton Beach Avenue, beside an alleyway back onto the boardwalk, we ascended the stairs to the subway overpass where I had left Tony the night before. There was an express train stopped temporarily at the station. We both took seats facing a window looking out over the Atlantic Ocean between the Soviet-style flat blocks. I looked into the expanse of its infinity. I contemplated last night, the days that followed, and then I thought on Tony.

'Do you still want to go back?' Tony asked.

'To Egypt or back in time?' I asked.

Tony shrugged.

I didn't speak. I looked at the Atlantic Ocean. I thought on whether the inclination to return would be with me always. Nothing in life is easy. I could sense that somewhere in the back of my mind, I was still there, in Alexandria of the 1930s. Somewhere in the multiverse, Sam(a) was still trying to speak to Wassim. Maybe in that universe, Sam(a) found a more respectable man who remained in the synagogue for the entirety of Shabbat services, married him, and had a great many children. Maybe I was the grandmother of a whole lot of people. Maybe in that universe, I became a revolutionary.

'Do you still want to go back?' Tony asked.

'Someday,' I said.

Somewhere in the multiverse, we would have been in Alexandria the following day. In the 21st century.

'I want to have dinner with you, tomorrow and the next day. I want to have lots of friends and a back yard and a large table at the centre of the back yard, where we talk about life and the world. And big holidays with tables surrounded by loved ones and your parents. And travel — I want to see the world with you,' I said.

'All we have is now,' Tony said.

I looked at him, speechless at first. I wondered if by this he meant to leave me on the other side of the subway door. And yet he was still holding my hand.

'All we have is now.'